MISSOURI VIGILANTES

General Sherlock has issued an order to exterminate the bandits of Taney County: shoot them like animals and hang all prisoners. So when sixteen-year-old Billy Stark falls into a trap and attempts to steal an army pay-roll, the military are hot on his trail. Fleeing for his life and burdened by a wounded companion, Billy faces extreme peril and is lured into a world where lynching, torture and bullets have replaced the law. Striving to maintain his morality, Billy finds himself drawn deeper into a web of evil . . .

MARK BANNERMAN

MISSOURI VIGILANTES

Complete and Unabridged

LINFORD
Leicester

First published in Great Britain in 2013 by
Robert Hale Limited
London

First Linford Edition
published 2015
by arrangement with
Robert Hale Limited
London

A catalogue record for this book is available
from the British Library.

ISBN 978–1–4448–2426–1

1

I guess I made a lot of bad mistakes when I was in Missouri in the 1880s. Looking back, I can make no excuses. My name is Billy Stark and when I was sixteen I saw Alfredo as a tough man but a kind one. He was Mexican and old enough to be my father. He befriended my mother when she needed help and he took me under his wing after she died. It never occurred to me to question what drove him through life or what the motives of those who followed him were. I remember the little things about him, like the frayed ends of his moustache and the smell of tobacco that always clung to him, and the rings that glinted on his fingers. Because I admired him, even loved him like the father I hadn't got, I was drawn along the path he was taking without fully comprehending just how wicked outlawry was. It all seemed a grand adventure until that fateful day in June 1883 when Alfredo met his nemesis.

The Missouri sun was shining warmly; mockingbirds trilled from the trees as we kept watch from the hillside flanking the Crescent Trail in Taney County. The trail came into view as it curved around a bluff, after which it stretched out towards the distant Fort Sibley. Boulder-strewn hills rose on each side, leading up to wooded crests.

There were eight of us — Alfredo, his six Mexican gang members whose names now elude me, and me. A nervous excitement was building in me because this was my first big job. Alfredo had told me that if it proved successful, there would be considerable financial reward for us all, but the truth was that I didn't care about money, just so long as I had enough to get by on. My sentiments revolved around the facts that I was among grown men and I was accepted as one of them, and for a 16-year-old that felt good.

I guess we were a ragged bunch, disinclined to wash apart from when we splashed across rivers. We all carried heavy Colt .44 pistols and I had practised for hours as Alfredo made plans for the job he had in mind. Except for yours truly, the gang were all heavily moustached and generally unshaven. As for me, I was already sprouting a beard. I was long and lean with my dark hair down to my shoulders and I guess I looked more mature than my tender years.

At that time I was unaware that General Sherlock, Commander of the District, had issued his order to exterminate the bandits of Taney County, to shoot them like animals and hang all prisoners.

Suddenly our lookout came rushing in to report that soldiers were approaching. Alfredo exchanged a meaningful nod with the rest of us and he said, 'Let's go, amigos!' at which we all hoisted our bandannas across our faces and fanned out to our pre-arranged positions behind boulders overlooking the trail — all of which seemed good places to open fire from.

I accompanied Alfredo as he crouched down behind a large boulder in a slight depression. We slid our rifles over the rock in front of us and waited for the soldiers to draw closer. Alfredo's opening shot was to be the signal for the rest of us to start firing.

Soon we heard the blowing of horses and the creak of wagon wheels and the little military cavalcade appeared from around the bluff.

I counted the blue-coated soldiers. They were mounted, riding abreast; an escort of two men in the front of the small white-canopied wagon, two men on the seat, and another two bringing up the rear. I assumed the paymaster would be inside the wagon, along with his cashbox, which contained the payroll of the isolated garrison at Fort Sibley — a payroll that was three months overdue.

All at once the sun seemed almighty hot and the birds had quieted. I felt sweat running down my face and there was a trembling in me that I couldn't quell.

Crazy as it seems, I clamped my eyes shut at that moment and listened to the creak of the wagon wheels as they came closer. When the sound seemed to fill my ears, I opened my eyes and took aim on one of the front riders. It was then that Alfredo's gun blasted off and was immediately followed by the other members of the gang opening up. I pressed my own trigger but the shot went wide. There was no time to fire again because a horrifying thing happened.

Under the hail of our bullets, the surviving members of the wagon's escort took flight, galloping further along the trail or back towards the bluff. The wagon slewed to a halt. Simultaneously a barrage of gunfire erupted from up the hill behind us, and my six Mexican *amigos* were utterly exposed. I saw three of them crumple down, shot in the back.

I risked a glance behind me and cried out in dismay. A great skirmish-line of soldiers had appeared from out of the trees and was advancing down towards us, their rifles spitting flame; the air was alive with spiteful lead. We'd been completely outflanked. Perhaps for the first time, Alfredo had walked into a trap.

The three gang members who had not so far been shot from the rear, rose from their now inadequate cover, and took to their heels down the slope, believing that the wagon itself posed little threat. But they were in for a shock. The canvas sides of the canopy were pulled up to reveal more bluecoats and two Gatling guns, which immediately belched a continuous stream of bullets. The Mexicans, my recent companions, rolled over and over like rag dolls, their bodies bloody, eventually coming to rest close to the wheels of the wagon.

As the gunfire died down, the exultant cries of the soldiers bludgeoned my ears.

Miraculously, when the bullets had been flying so perilously above our heads, Alfredo and I had been shielded by a slight rise in the ground behind us, whilst we'd been protected from the Gatlings by our original boulder cover.

Alfredo hissed, 'Stay still, Billy,' as we heard approaching boots pounding the ground behind us.

I lay with my face in the earth, holding my breath, Alfredo's crushing body shielding me, the aroma of his baccy filling my nostrils. He must have noticed that my teeth were chattering with fear.

It seemed inevitable that we would be discovered, that we might be dead within seconds. But to my relief the thud of boots and the clink of weapons suddenly lessened and I realized that the soldiers must have broken their skirmish line and circled the depression in which we sheltered. They were heading down to join their comrades on the trail. I started to breathe again.

'What are we gonna do?' I whispered to Alfredo.

'Till the bluebellies move on, we stay here,' he responded. 'But maybe they come back to pick up the bodies. Just pray that they don't come near us. If they do, we'll have to fight for our lives.'

I nodded. I figured that it would be better to die alongside Alfredo than to die alone.

By the time the military had re-formed around the wagon, the escorts, who had galloped off, returned. We could hear the shouted commands of the non-coms.

Alfredo removed his hat and, with utmost caution, raised his head to peer over the boulder while I waited anxiously for the verdict.

'Some bluebellies have climbed the slope,' he murmured. 'They're takin' the bodies back to the wagon.' He dropped his face into his ring-encrusted hands, then said, 'Thees has been the worst day in my life.'

'Will the soldiers come this way?' I asked.

He shook his head with uncertainty. 'We're safe for the moment. The rest of 'em have formed up on the trail. I theenk they get ready to move out.

When they're gone, we'll get away.'

I realized there was a quiver in his voice. He was choked with emotion. I could see that tears glistened on his cheeks, tears caused by the fury that his plans had come to nothing and his men had been massacred.

I stayed silent, my brain churning over the terrible events of the past hours. Then I got around to thinking how Alfredo had turned up at our homestead near the town of Branson a year ago, how he'd helped my ma by cutting up wood, feeding the hogs, milking the cows, tending the goats and countless other chores. I knew he'd been attracted to Ma and she'd been so happy to have him around. With only me as a companion, she'd been kind of restless since Pa had walked out. I, too, was glad that Alfredo was with us. He treated me like a grown-up and taught me many things about the ways of the world. But then Ma had taken ill with pneumonia and through those awful days we'd watched helplessly as she got worse. Alfredo nursed her with amazing compassion and tenderness for a man so rugged in appearance. The doctor came frequently but there was nothing he could do for her. Finally she passed away. We buried her on the hill overlooking the homestead. I sat by the grave for a whole night before I said my final farewell.

Alfredo sold off our livestock and gave me the money, refusing to take anything for the work he'd put in.

When he'd said he would have to move on, I'd wept. I guess I'd had visions of him staying on and us working the smallholding together like father and son. But I could see he was quite determined to leave, and this created in me such despair, such a fear of lonesomeness, that I pleaded with him to let me go with him. He was reluctant to agree, even confiding in me that he was wanted by the law and that he was going to meet up with his gang, but this in no way deterred me and eventually he conceded.

★　★　★

Now, he rested his hand on my shoulder.

'I'm sorry, Billy,' he said, 'sorry I get you into thees mess.'

'We're lucky,' I said. 'At least we're still livin'.'

He nodded.

High in the sky I could see two picket-winged buzzards circling. Then we heard the creak of wagon wheels coming from down on the trail and the renewed shouts of the non-coms. The hope rose in me that the soldiers were pulling out.

Alfredo risked a further glance over the boulder and I saw the tension cut through him.

'Are they leavin'?' I gasped.

He didn't answer at first, then he cursed. 'Main bunch are marchin' out,' he said, 'but they leave behind maybe six men. They're comin' up the slope now!' He unholstered his big Colt .44.

11

2

I can only assume that the soldiers who now inadvertently approached us were heading back to the original spot where they'd camped. Their intention was probably to collect the equipment that had been left behind. But it didn't make much difference what their intention was because by the way Alfredo was reacting I guessed they were heading straight for us. This time there was no chance that they would bypass the depression.

With lips close to my ear, Alfredo hissed, 'When I say go, we come out firin', gun down as many as we can.'

'Sure,' I nodded, thumbing back the hammer of my pistol and curling my finger around the trigger. Suddenly a voice inside me was screaming out, 'Kill or be killed!' completely overriding my other senses.

We could hear the casual conversation of the soldiers getting closer. Seconds elapsed, then Alfredo yelled, 'Go!' and we sprang from our shelter like a couple of catamounts, our guns unleashing a barrage of fire. This time we had the surprise. For a fleeting moment, I glimpsed the horrified faces of the soldiers, but then our bullets tore into them and they went down. The two survivors turned tail and fled down the hill in giant strides.

Alfredo took aim at their retreating backs, but then changed his mind and lowered his gun. I'll never know why he showed that mercy. I don't think he was a killer through and through.

'Let's get out o' here!' he cried, and now it was our turn to run. Gathering up our rifles we mounted the hill. I was afraid the main military column might have heard the shots and would return to investigate. We ran until our breath was heaving. A brief pause and then we hurried on. When we reached the trees, I glanced back and grunted with dismay.

The blue of uniforms had appeared on the trail. The fleeing survivors of our onslaught joined them — but now Alfredo urged me into the timber. We clawed our way through foliage and brush. Panic gnawed at my heels.

'Pray to God that the horses are still there,' Alfredo panted.

We had left our animals hobbled in a clearing a mile or so away from the point of our intended ambush, fearing that if they were closer they might alert the military horses. As we paused once more, we heard the unmistakable sounds of pursuit, of men rushing through the trees.

Alfredo cursed as we continued. I was nigh on exhausted, my legs close to giving out, and a stitch stabbed into my side. Gritting my teeth against the pain, I stumbled in Alfredo's wake. Several times he glanced back, calling to me to keep going, that we had almost reached the horses . . . if, pray God, they were where we had left them.

I tried my utmost to drive myself on,

but suddenly my legs seemed to dissolve beneath me and I collapsed. I tried to get up, only to fall back. Alfredo was immediately at my side. He hesitated, then gathered me up in his brawny arms and carried me until we reached the clearing. To our relief the horses were still there, cropping unconcernedly at the grass.

I was lowered to the ground and was sufficiently recovered to follow Alfredo's example of finding my saddle and blanket, cached at the side, throwing them across the back of my black mare and drawing the cinch tight. With trembling fingers I unbuckled the animal's hobbles, got my foot into the stirrup and hauled myself up. Alfredo was already astride his mount and he waved us forward.

But as we heel-rammed our animals into motion, there came an almighty racket of excited cries from behind us and, glancing over my shoulder, I saw several bluebellies disgorging from the trees.

I snatched my pistol from its holster

and blazed off a shot in their direction. There was no time to see if I'd found a target. I struggled to control my mare; she had started to rear. Her front hoofs hit the ground as the rattle of gunfire sounded from behind and my hat was plucked from my head by whining lead. There was no time to retrieve it. I sent my mount pounding after Alfredo's big roan, kicking madly with my heels, and we crashed through undergrowth on to the forest track up which we'd come earlier that day. More shots cracked out from behind, but they went wide.

Alfredo was setting a murderous pace, but we'd raced no more than a half-mile, when he veered from the trail and up through the trees, our horses slowing as the incline became steeper. When we emerged at the crest of the hill, renewed apprehension hammered at me.

We drew rein on the lip of a deep ravine some fifteen feet across. I could see a river, glistening like a silver ribbon in its depths.

'We jump,' Alfredo panted. 'It's our best chance.'

Cold dread gnawed at my guts. 'The horses are exhausted,' I argued. 'They'll never make it!'

'Billy,' he snapped at me as he'd never done before. 'It ees our only chance. We will jump!'

I knew he was angry with me. But then we both heard the rustling of foliage from behind us. If our pursuers were still on foot, they must have followed us at a headlong pace.

I realized he was right. Jumping was our only chance. 'Let's go!'

He reined his horse back to get a good run-up. Then he kicked him into motion and the big roan took off like Pegasus, sailing gamely over the gorge and landing safely on the far side.

I swallowed hard, edged the mare back so she was prepared for the jump. At least, I thought she was. I'd tasted fear a-plenty that day, but this seemed more awesome than anything that had gone before. From the opposite rim

Alfredo beckoned me frantically but all I could think about was the river so far below.

I rammed hard with my heels, screamed a rebel yell and we charged forward. At the moment when she should have jumped, the mare baulked, pulling up with her forelegs stiff, and I was thrown from her back. Had I not kept my grip on the reins, I would have toppled over the edge, but I somehow maintained my hold and hauled myself to safe ground.

The mare was snorting, the whites of her eyes radiating panic. She reared, unleashing a whinny, but I calmed her and led her back for another attempt. I climbed into the saddle. I was trembling like an aspen. I urged her forward again.

When she again baulked at the rim, I had not learned from previous experience. Having come to an even more abrupt halt than previously, she reared, snorting. This time I fell backwards from the saddle, landing flat on my back, knocking the breath from my body. When, winded, I raised my head, I was just in time to see the mare landing gracefully on the far side of gorge, close to where Alfredo sat his horse. To achieve the leap she hadn't even taken a run-up.

I felt totally furious with myself; I had placed not only myself in danger of being caught by our pursuers, but Alfredo as well. However, if he also was angry at my stupidity, he didn't show it. Without hesitation, he heeled his roan into motion and jumped back to my side, shouting at me to clamber up behind him. This I did, getting my arms around his midriff and hanging on for dear life. The big roan took the return jump in his stride, and I thanked God he was a strong animal.

Once over, I slid to the ground, grabbed the reins of my recalcitrant mare and climbed into the saddle. We moved off immediately, but before we could reach the cover of trees, a volley of shots crashed out from the side we'd just vacated and I felt something clip my upper arm. But I knew it wasn't serious. I glanced over my shoulder, saw soldiers aiming their guns to fire again, but before the second volley came we were shielded by the timber. Soon, we were in full flight, the low-hanging fronds snatching at us as we plunged through. Dusk was now sifting down through the branches.

Sure enough, our pursuers were on foot and would be unable to get across the ravine. We had thus gained a temporary respite.

I realized that it was my stupidity and clumsiness that had brought us so close to disaster. For a minute I was blinded by my shame; then I noticed how Alfredo was slumped forward and swaying in his saddle, and my shame turned to horror.

Suddenly he dropped from his horse, landing heavily. With his foot hooked in the stirrup he was dragged for several yards before he came free, then he lay perfectly still.

3

I hauled my mare to a skidding halt, slid to the ground and dropped down at Alfredo's side. His shirt front was glistening with blood and his eyes were closed. I thought he was dead, but then he groaned and moved his hand to his chest, his palm against the hole from which the blood seeped.

I guess I panicked, a feeling of hopelessness swamping me. What the hell could I do without him? However I suddenly recalled how he'd saved me, jumping back over the ravine when he could have galloped on. This somehow calmed my senses, enabled me to think more logically.

I got my hands beneath his armpits and dragged him into a sitting position; my hands were slippery with blood.

I pulled off my vest. I unbuttoned my shirt and shrugged out of it. I slipped it around Alfredo, tying the sleeves behind his back and padding it up as best I could over the wound. I prayed that it would stem the bleeding.

And now his eyes were open. He groaned through clamped teeth, then his lips moved.

'Billy, you go on . . . get away. I'm finished . . . leave me . . . '

'No,' I snapped back. 'Got to get you to a doctor. I'll help you onto your horse. I'll mount behind you, hold you steady.'

He cursed, said my name, and then trailed off.

I left him then and rounded up the horses. I fixed the mare to the roan with a lead-rope.

It was one of the hardest tasks of my life to get Alfredo astride the roan. Thinking back, considering the state he was in, I don't know where I found the strength to do it. All the time, he was gasping with the terrible pain he suffered, but he showed courage, too. Maybe he realized it was the only chance he had for survival.

Once he was mounted, I climbed up behind him. I got my arms around his midriff, somehow holding him steady, but this was difficult because wherever I touched him, he gasped with the hurt, and when we edged forward the gait of the horse over the uneven ground brought further suffering.

I had to decide where to head for, and in the now-descended gloom any journey would be difficult. I figured the town of Coltville was the nearest and I knew there was a doctor there, though whether Alfredo would be alive when we arrived was uncertain.

I knew I had to set a course to the north-west, when I would hit the Brokebridge Road. Alfredo lapsed into deep, ragged breaths and I took satisfaction from these as I knew he was still surviving. We travelled as fast as we could, firstly through forest and then along the deserted road. On several occasions Alfredo nearly slipped from the horse but somehow I held on to him, restoring him to a more stable position.

I lost count of time. I was utterly weary and the horses were wearing thin. I became aware of movement in the meadows to my side, but it was only the tall grass made restless by the breeze.

The tortuous hours of that night dragged on and on and our stops to rest became more frequent. The moon had disappeared, leaving only the stone-cold stars to light the sky. A ground mist swirled up, rump-high to the horses. At last we reached the decrepit bridge that had earned the road its name. It was patched up and I went across it, thanking God that we were finally nearing the town.

Soon we were passing through outlying cabins, seeing no life apart from a couple of dogs. When we entered the main street, the whole town seemed curled up in sleep, no light showing, apart from that from the stars.

I thought: How the hell am I going to

find the doctor with nobody to ask?

We passed the hostelry, shrouded in gloom. Then we reached the closed saloon and I glimpsed a man sprawled on the stoop, obviously a drunk.

'Where's the doctor's place?' I called to him.

His head jerked up. 'Eh?' he grunted.

I repeated the question.

'Piss off!' he mumbled and his head dropped down to the boards.

I growled with frustration. Then an idea came to me. Maybe I was taking a chance but I could think of nothing better. I drew my pistol and triggered off three quick shots into the sky, shattering the street's quiet and immediately causing the high-pitched yapping of dogs from the shadows.

Lights flared in several first-floor buildings. From the upstairs of the saloon, an awry-haired woman, clearly a sporting lady, raised her window and poked her head out. 'What in tarnation are you doin'?' she screeched.

'We need the doctor real bad.

Where's his place?'

'Go to hell!' she called. 'No right to disturb the peace at this time o' night.' She gave me a quizzical look for I was still bare-chested and hatless and Alfredo clearly presented a sorry sight.

She withdrew her head, but then the image of what she'd seen must have registered with her because she reappeared and said, 'Doc Wilmer . . . second house from the end of the street. On the right. He's been on a bender, drunk as a lord!'

I thanked her and set the horses in motion.

It was as we rode that a sudden fear hit me. I couldn't hear Alfredo's wheezing breath — but then to my utter astonishment, he spoke. 'Billy, I can't go further. I'm done for.'

'No you're not,' I countered. 'We'll have the doc patchin' you up in no time.'

If he's not too drunk, I thought.

Alfredo went quiet again, too weak to argue. But to survive as long as he had gave me hope. He was one tough *hombre*.

Doc Wilmer's house looked run-down and weather-beaten, and was surrounded by weeds. I reined in the roan in front of it. I dismounted and then, as gently as I could, I lowered Alfredo from the saddle, nigh collapsing under his considerable weight. Somehow, I got him to the house's stoop and rested him down. His shirt and pants were shining with blood. He slumped, doubled over, sucking in deep lungfuls of air.

The house was in darkness. I rang the bell twice, but there was no answer. I decided to gain access from the back and went around the side wall.

To my surprise the latch was up on the kitchen door and it swung open as I touched it. I entered. A stench of rancid coffee grounds filled my nostrils. I groped along a hallway to the foot of a stair-case. It was then I heard a thick snoring coming from upstairs. I followed the sound, climbing to the landing, to the

main bedroom. I paused in the doorway.

The thin light of pre-dawn was
seeping through the window and I
could see the man I guessed was the
doctor lying among crumpled blankets,
fully dressed in his frock coat and
boots. The air was thick with whiskey
fumes.

I moved across the room and raised
the blind.

The doctor's string tie was hanging
undone on his chest and unshaven
stubble was thick upon his jaw. His
mouth was lolled open, quivering to
accommodate his snoring.

I cursed. This wasn't what I'd
anticipated. With Alfredo out on the
front stoop, possibly dying, I felt I
couldn't waste time. Surely an intoxi-
cated medic was better than none at all.
I grabbed his shoulder and gave it a
firm shake.

He grunted, snorting and tossing his
head. His hands clawed the blankets,
then his eyelids twitched up.

'Don't worry,' I hissed. 'I ain't gonna do you no harm, Doc.'

There was a long pause. His brow was wrinkled as he attempted to absorb the situation. Finally, he gingerly sat up, shrugging off my hand from his shoulder. 'Who the hell are you?' he demanded in a surprisingly firm voice.

'My name's Billy,' I confided, 'and my friend's in sore need o' your professional help.'

'Come back at surgery time,' he said.

'No, that'll be too late. I need you right now . . . '

'You in trouble with the law?' he asked.

'Only if they catch me,' I said, and now I was getting impatient. 'My friend's outside. Help me get him some place where you can examine him.'

'I'll be arrested for this,' he complained. 'I never treat cases like this.'

I drew my gun and pointed it at him. 'But you'll treat this case,' I said, baring my teeth in a snarl. 'You can say you were threatened with a gun.'

'All r-right. All right,' he stammered, 'but let's be civilized about this.'

He emitted a sigh of relief as I slipped my gun back into its holster.

I offered him a hand and hauled him onto his feet. He was unsteady but he followed me down the stairs, then out through the front door and onto the stoop. Alfredo was still slumped where I'd left him and he glanced up with a look of hopelessness.

Somehow we lifted him onto his feet and helped him into the house. A moment later we were in Wilmer's surgery — a small room lined with shelves of labelled jars. We got Alfredo onto the couch.

'I need some light,' the doctor said and he fetched a lamp from the washstand and fired the wick with a match. 'Help me get his shirt off,' he said.

Alfredo was groaning as we peeled away his bloodstained shirt and the makeshift bandage I'd fashioned. Flesh came away where the flannel had adhered to the wound.

Alfredo was sweating; he sat with his head down.

Wilmer fetched a bowl of water and gently sponged away congealed blood from the ragged bullet hole in the right side of Alfredo's upper chest. Then he probed the wound with his long fingers. For a drunk, his touch was surprisingly steady. Maybe that was the sign of a true professional.

'He's haemorrhaged badly,' he commented.

'Well?' I queried. 'Can you operate?'

'I could try to get the bullet out, but there's no guarantee he'll live through it. There'd be plenty of pain. I don't have anaesthetic.'

'But you'll do it?' I persisted. 'I'll pay you.' I knew that there was money in my hip pocket.

He pursed his lips, hiccupped and sighed. Then he nodded.

4

I guess deep inside me there must be a streak of squeamishness, because at that moment, as Doc Wilmer fetched his instruments and placed a thin wooden splint between Alfredo's lips for him to bite on, I felt a desperate need to circulate. In fact it seemed a wise thing to take a look outside and make certain that no members of the military had trailed us to the town.

I saw Wilmer set to work with a needle-fine probe and heard Alfredo's gasp of pain. That was when I turned away.

I realized we must have left tracks a blind man could follow.

'I'll be back,' I said and I quit the surgery. Call me a coward if you will.

I went out to the porch, thankful to inhale the cool air. Dawn was creeping in, like a pearl-grey cat slinking down from the distant mountains. From somewhere in the background a cockerel crowed.

I glanced up the street. Only a few folks were about and there was no sign of any military.

My gaze drifted to the horses, still waiting patiently where they'd been hitched. Their eyes looked at me reproachfully. I went to them and untied them. I recalled we'd passed the hostelry when we'd ridden in and I decided to make for it. As I led the animals away, I heard Alfredo's shout of agony coming from the window. I walked on, feeling sick.

The town was stirring to life by the time I reached the hostelry. Its big doors were flung open and I entered, wondering if anybody was about. The place was lit by several oil lamps and the scent of horse ordure and nitrogen filled the air. I called, 'Hi there!' and glanced around, seeing the horses, who were aware of my presence, blowing and moving restlessly in their stalls. Then a surprising thing happened.

'Howdy, mister. What can I do for you?' A young girl, about my age, stepped from the shadows, holding a curry comb. I gasped with astonishment. She was wearing a blue overall and her blonde hair was curled into ringlets. I guess I was struck dumb because she was as pretty as morning sunshine.

'My daddy's not well,' she explained, 'so I'm helpin' out.' Her eyes lingered on mine and there was a look of surprise on her face. 'You know,' she added, 'you're so like my brother Greg was.'

'Your b-brother?' I stammered.

'Yes,' she said, and her voice was sad. 'He died last year. Killed when his friend's gun went off accidentally.'

'That was real bad,' I said. Then I realized what I'd come here for. 'My horses. They need oats and water.'

'I'll fix that,' she said, and she reached out and took hold of the reins. But she didn't lead the horses off right away. We just stood there, looking at each other, not knowing what to say. She didn't seem any more anxious to break off our acquaintanceship than I was.

'You're a stranger in Coltville?' she eventually managed.

I nodded. 'Brought my friend in to get some treatment from Doc Wilmer.'

I was aware that I was still shirtless, having used mine to bandage Alfredo.

'Have you a shirt for sale?' I inquired.

She smiled. 'Not for sale,' she said. 'It'll be a gift. There's an old one of mine out the back. I'll fetch it.'

'Won't it be a bit small for me?' I queried.

She snorted indignantly and said, 'I'm not exactly small,' and we both laughed.

'I'll see to the horses and get the shirt,' she said. She led the horses into the stalls and carried two buckets of oats to them. Then she disappeared out the back.

I stood waiting. My thoughts swung to Alfredo and the pain he must be going through. I shouldn't have left him. I ought to get back.

The girl returned and handed me the shirt. I pulled it on, feeling her eyes on me. The shirt was loose-fitting.

'Is it OK?' she asked.

'Sure, and thanks,' I nodded. 'I must get back to my friend now.'

'What's your name?' she said.

'Billy.'

'Mine's Jessaka . . . Jessaka Sheldrake. Say, Billy, I noticed blood on the saddle of the roan. You on the run? From the law, I mean.'

I was taken aback. What could I say?

She answered for me. 'You are. I can tell. And you've been wounded. I saw blood on your arm. Let me bathe it and patch you up.'

'No,' I said. 'I've got to get back.'

As I turned she said, 'But you'll come again.'

'I will . . . I will,' and I meant it. I turned to go, my mind now filled with guilt at having left Alfredo for so long.

There were several people about as I hurried back down the street, but they all ignored me. I reached the doctor's house and entered through the front door. All seemed silent. A light showed from the doorway of the surgery, and suddenly Doc Wilmer appeared, his face as gaunt as winter.

'Bad news,' he said. 'Your friend didn't survive the operation. He died as I tried to get the bullet out. There was nothin' I could do.'

'He's dead?' I gasped. I should have expected it, but now I couldn't believe that Alfredo was gone.

'Like I told you,' Wilmer went on, 'there was nothin' I could do. Nobody could've saved him. You better come in and see for yourself.'

Alfredo was lying face up on the couch, his chest a whole mess of blood. He had clearly passed on to the next world.

Horror sliced through my guts.

I looked at Wilmer, saw the strange light in his eyes and guessed at the truth. 'You killed him,' I cried out. 'You meant it that way all along.'

He said, 'That's a mighty awful thing

to say, but it doesn't matter. You'll have somethin' else to think about now.'

And right then, the voice sounded from behind me. 'Keep your hands away from your gun, kid! Now raise your arms.'

The breath died in my throat. I turned and saw the man with a badge pinned to his vest. He'd been standing behind the door. His gun was pointed at my chest.

I raised my hands, knowing I had no option.

'Let me introduce you,' Wilmer slurred. 'This is Marshal Henshaw and he doesn't tolerate no-good kids.'

Right at that moment I kind of froze inside. A voice kept pounding in my head: Alfredo's dead . . . Alfredo's dead. It didn't seem to matter what happened to me now.

'Let's take a walk to the jail,' Henshaw said, and he stepped forward, still keeping me covered; he removed my Colt from its holster and tucked it in his belt.

I exchanged a scornful glance with

Doc Wilmer, and then I was marched down the stairs with the marshal's gun at my back. Despite the early hour, there was now plenty of life in the street and folks stared at us as we proceeded to the marshal's office with its adjoining jail. A couple of deputies were there, sipping coffee. I was soon pushed into a cell.

'The army'll be comin' to pick you up,' Henshaw explained as he turned the key. 'They'll know how to deal with you.'

I slumped onto the wooden bunk. There were tears in my eyes. My whole world seemed to have imploded.

Later, from the conversation I overheard, I learned the military were coming to collect me the next day. After that, I dreaded what would happen. My mood deepened still further when one of the deputies, a man called Sligo, taunted me with a copy of the *Coltville Times*. He laughed as I read the front page: 'General Sherlock, Commander of the District, has issued orders to exterminate the bandits of Taney County, to shoot them like animals and hang all prisoners.'

Through that long, dreary day, remorse settled over me like a suffocating blanket. I kept thinking of Alfredo. Had it not been for the delay I'd caused him when we'd jumped the ravine, he wouldn't have been shot. Had I not insisted on getting him to a doctor, he might yet be alive. I'd done what I'd thought was best for him, and everything had gone sour. Now, it seemed I was headed for a hang-rope and, like a drowning man, my past life swam into my brain.

I recalled how I'd been happy enough when I was growing up. I never had any brothers or sisters, but I didn't miss them because my ma and pa gave me all the companionship I needed. Our homestead was too remote to attend the schoolhouse, and Ma had tutored me every day, stimulating in me an interest in the classics and giving me a good knowledge of English and numbers.

Pa took me out hunting and exploring, and taught me how to handle a gun and ride a horse. I looked up to him and figured I was lucky to have him for my father.

At first I didn't take much notice of the bickering and rowing that went on between my parents, but eventually not even a kid of twelve could miss the fact that they were not happy together. Then came the awful time when Pa wasn't there any more. Ma told me that he'd left us and wouldn't be coming back. She said they just couldn't tolerate each other any longer. Apparently he had another woman.

For a long while, I watched for him, figuring she might have been wrong in saying he wouldn't return, but the months turned into years and gradually I convinced myself that I had lost my pa. Maybe I should have been bitter about the way he'd walked out, leaving us after all those years, but I couldn't bring myself to hate him.

As I grew, I tried to take his place,

doing the chores around the homestead. I spent long hours out hunting,
bringing home a plentiful supply of
meat. But over the next hard-working
years, Ma weakened, and after a while,
she became ill frequently. Eventually,
when she took to her bed, wracked by a
terrible cough, I called a doctor and
saw from his grim expression that the
prospects were not good.

Then, one morning, Alfredo showed
up and to me he seemed like an angel
coming down from heaven. Without
being asked, he set to work, helping me
with chopping wood, tending our crop
field and feeding the livestock. I can't
recall how exactly it came about, but he
moved in with us and was soon so good
to have around that Ma's health
seemed to improve. Before long she was
up and about, appearing as happy as a
songbird. It was somehow typical of
Alfredo, for his mere presence, with his
good humour and kindness, brightened
our lives. I knew he took a shine to Ma,
just as she did to him. But then came

the time when she became ill again, and now it was much worse than it had been before. She became deathly pale and thin. Her eyes sank deep into her skull. Not even Alfredo could make her better, although he tried hard enough.

Tears streamed down my cheeks as I recalled her final days.

* * *

As I remained trapped in that cell, time dragged torturously. Through the bars, I had a clear view of the office, and I watched deputies come and go as they undertook their duties. I was completely ignored, apart from when I was given a plateful of beans and a hunk of bread, followed by a mug of coffee. I was also marched out to the closet for a brief visit.

As evening closed in I lay on the wooden bunk. There was no mattress and just a single moth-eaten blanket. As I sank deeper and deeper into depression, I must have dozed, for I was suddenly standing on a scaffold and a hood had been placed over my head. With rough, hard hands, somebody rammed a noose around my neck; I could smell the clean heavy tang of the rope's creosote. Its coil was tightening, constricting my windpipe.

Before I could snatch a final breath, the trap-door collapsed beneath my feet; I plunged down and my neck snapped with a crack.

5

I awoke with a shout, sweat streaming down my face, and Deputy Sligo, seated at the desk in the outer office, yelled at me to keep quiet. 'Ain't no point in you wakin' the neighbourhood! The army'll be here to pick you up in the mornin'. They'll take you back to Fort Sibley. They got a fine gallows there.'

I stood up from the bunk, gripped the bars and strained against them. They didn't give an inch. The only other outlet from the cell was a window and that, too, was barred. I didn't know why, because it was so small a beaver couldn't have squeezed through.

I returned to the bunk and lay down, gritting my teeth with chagrin. I couldn't sleep this time. I remained awake for hours, seeing the darkness take hold through the window. For a while I listened to folks moving along the street outside, together with the creak of wagons and the plod of horses. Presently, things quieted.

Sligo had gone off duty and another deputy, a man with a mop of white hair, took his place. He gave me a quick glance to ensure I was still alive, after which he sat cleaning his rifle in the glow of an oil lamp, and whistling through his teeth.

I didn't know what the time was; it seemed pretty late, when the outer door of the office rattled open and the first thing I noticed was a familiar voice — very familiar. 'Evenin', Mister Lowry,' she said.

It was the girl from the hostelry, Jessaka Sheldrake. She had entered the office and was standing at the deputy's desk, not sparing a glance in my direction. She was wearing a pretty bonnet and a dress, and she was holding a basket.

'Well, my dear,' Deputy Lowry said, 'what can I do for you?'

'Ma sent me over with some vittles

for the prisoner,' she explained. 'Can't understand why. I reckon all bandits are scum and should be exterminated, but Ma feels sorry for anybody behind bars and usually sends over somethin' for them.'

'Yes, I know,' Lowry nodded.

I guess I was struck dumb, shocked into silence by what she had said. She sounded so positively forthright that I felt she was expressing her true sentiments. I stood, grasping the bars, sick to the roots of my soul.

She started to unpack items from her basket, placing them on the desk.

'And she sent an apple pie over for you, Mister Lowry.'

'Why, tell your ma a big thank you,' he said.

'This one's for you,' she said. 'The smaller pie's for the prisoner, though I'm sure he doesn't deserve it. I'll just step across and give it to him.'

'No, no, don't worry,' Lowry said. 'I'll give it to him later on. Wouldn't want you to mix up with a bad'un like him.'

'That's no problem,' she insisted. 'I'll — '

'I'll give him the pie,' he interrupted in a firm voice, and she backed down.

'Well, don't eat it yourself,' she said with a laugh.

'I won't. I'll give it to him. That's for sure.'

She said, 'Good night, Mister Lowry,' and she left without a single backward glance at me.

Lowry unwrapped his pie and was soon tucking in, making slapping noises with his lips. When he was finished he belched, and I saw how his eyes rested on the package that contained my pie and the other goodies that Mrs Sheldrake had kindly sent.

'You promised to give it to me,' I called to him.

He snapped out of his reverie and stood up. He shook the package, then moved over to me and passed it through the bars. 'Good job I'm honest,' he said and returned to his desk.

I sat down on the bunk. I felt kind of

trembly inside. The sight of Jessaka, looking so cute in bonnet and dress, had stirred me. But her words had hit me like bee stings. I was utterly puzzled.

I unwrapped the pie, and along with it was an assortment of biscuits and a cake with a cherry on the top. I ate the cake; it was really good. The pie looked equally tempting. I went to take a bite from it, and my teeth clamped against something metallic. I was puzzled. I probed into the pie with my finger and uncovered the barrel of a small gun. My heart began to beat faster. I glanced across to make sure Lowry's attention was turned away from me. His head was rested down upon his arms; he was obviously taking a nap. I probed some more, wiped away some apple, and extracted the gun. It was a derringer, a twin-barrelled pocket pistol, and it was primed with two shells. Taped to it was a note. I unfolded it and my eyes seized upon the neat handwriting.

Billy,

I hope this will help you escape during the night.

I will have your horse saddled and ready at the hostelry.

Good luck.

Yours,

Jessaka

PS Trust you don't have to hurt Mr Lowry.

I swallowed hard. So Jessaka hadn't meant those bad things she'd said. I wished I could take her in my arms and thank her. Maybe she'd be waiting at the hostelry. But now I would have to be very careful if I was to get away.

Lowry had started to snore. I decided to wait an hour. Then, hopefully, all the townsfolk would be in bed and the streets would be deserted.

I lay on the bunk, feigning sleep in case Lowry checked. Thoughts of Jessaka filled my mind. We'd met only briefly, but it was long enough for something special to pass between us, like a communion of spirits. I'd never had a real girlfriend; now, perhaps, everything would change — that was, if I managed to escape.

I waited for what seemed an eternity. Lowry had awakened and was scribbling away at some paperwork.

Silently, I eased off the safety catch on the derringer.

That was when the outer door of the office rattled open again and Sligo came in. I groaned with dismay. One opponent I might be able to get the better of, but not two.

'Well,' I heard Lowry say, 'how come you're back here at this time of night?'

Sligo cursed, then said, 'The old woman kicked me out of bed. Said she had a headache. Threw my clothes out the window.'

Lowry chuckled. 'If you intend to stay here for an hour or two, I might as well go home. Prisoner's asleep, I guess.'

'Please yourself,' Sligo said.

Five minutes later, Lowry departed.

Sligo came and peered in at me, then returned to his chair.

I decided to play my hand. 'Mrs Sheldrake sent me over some pie and biscuits. I'm right full of pie. D'you want the biscuits?'

At first he didn't seem to hear, but then he looked in my direction. 'Don't want your leftovers, kid,' he said. I cursed inwardly. Perhaps a minute went by, then he seemed to have a change of heart. 'Maybe I'll make myself some coffee. A biscuit will go down well enough with that.'

I watched as he set the kettle on the stove to boil, then he came towards me. My nerves were yammering wildly. This was probably the only chance I would get.

Holding the derringer behind me in my right hand, I offered the biscuits to him with my left. I drew back slightly, causing him to reach through the bars to get them. I dropped the biscuits, grabbed his coat sleeve and pressed the muzzle of the pistol against his forehead.

He uttered a shocked, gurgling sound. 'What the . . . ?'

'The keys to this cell are on the desk,' I shouted at him. 'Get them, bring them back. I'll have you covered all the way. One false move and I'll shoot.'

He cursed me to hell, hesitated, then he gave a grudging nod and said, 'Don't shoot. I'll get 'em.'

I released his sleeve, he turned and I watched him walk slowly to the desk and pick up the keys.

Suddenly he erupted into life, lashing out with his arm to send the oil lamp flying. I fired the derringer and heard him yell with pain as he thudded to the floor. Flame from the lamp was taking hold, catching on to the carpet, licking up over the desk.

Sligo was sprawled on the ground, groaning and clutching his side.

'Throw the keys over to me,' I yelled. 'I'll plug you again if you try any tricks!'

He looked across at me. Flames were rising about him. He was dead scared. I could see it in his eyes.

With seemingly great effort, he drew his arm back and threw the keys in my direction. They landed short, but I reached through the bars and clawed on to them. There were four keys on the ring. My hands were shaking as I tried them, one after the other, in the cell's lock. At the third attempt the key slid into place. I turned it and pushed the door open.

For the moment I discounted Sligo. He'd slumped over again and I guessed he was pretty badly wounded. But I had no time to speculate. I grabbed the kettle from the stove and emptied it on to the flames. Then I went to work. I grabbed the carpet, smothered the flames from it and used it and my feet to quell the remaining fire.

I grabbed Sligo's shoulders and dragged him across the office to the cell. He was as limp as a sackful of oats and just as heavy. I dumped him through the door and locked him in. Only then did he start to complain, saying he was gut-shot and dying and I couldn't be so inhuman as to leave him. He said the flames might start up again and he'd be trapped.

'If you're dyin',' I said, 'it won't make no difference.'

I left the keys on the desk. This was probably a mistake but I didn't give it much thought. At the same time I noticed my gun-belt on a side shelf. I grabbed it, buckled it on, and made for the door. A second later I was outside in the cool night air.

6

I glanced around and satisfied myself that there was nobody about. The gunshot and fire appeared to have gone unnoticed. I set off along the shadowy sidewalk and within a few minutes I was approaching the hostelry. The prospect that I might soon be with Jessaka again excited me.

The hostelry was in complete darkness, but the big door was slightly ajar. I entered and the familiar aroma of horses assailed me. I paused, listening, but the only sound was the restless movement of the animals in their stalls. Jessaka had said that my horse would be saddled and ready, but in the gloom there was no sign of it.

I took a pace forward and that was when the man's voice cut through the silence. 'Stay where you are, Stark, and raise your hands. I got you covered.'

I cursed. This was the second time within twenty-four hours that I'd been outsmarted in this way. The threat had come from the shadows to my left. I debated whether to throw myself to the side and snatch my gun from its holster, but then I recalled that, in my haste to leave the marshal's office, I hadn't reloaded it.

I lifted my hands.

A match scraped and a lamp flared into light. Now I saw the man who was covering me with his rifle. His hair was grey and he was thin and clad in an overall. I guessed he was the hostler, Jessaka's father.

As my own face was illuminated he jerked with surprise and whispered, 'My God . . . it's Greg!'

'I'm not Greg,' I said. 'I know he's dead.'

'Well, you're sure-fire like 'im,' he said. 'I guess you busted out of jail. I was sure you'd show up here sooner or later. You're a fool to have got on the wrong side of the law. It's my duty to hand you back to the marshal.'

'The military'll hang me for sure,' I said. 'How come you knew about me?'

'I found out my daughter had stolen my derringer. She was a stupid girl to do what she did. Her mother told me about it. They never figured I was well enough to take any action, but I was and I believe in upholdin' the law.'

For all his words, I could see there was doubt wavering in his eyes. He was not a hard man. I gambled on him not pulling the trigger.

'I need to get away,' I said, and I stepped forward. I watched his eyes, fearing he might shoot me. But I got my hands on the barrel of his rifle and he allowed me to lift it from his grasp.

'Damn!' he growled. 'I ain't no shootin' man.'

I leaned the rifle against the wall and said, 'There's a fella with a bullet wound locked in the cell at the marshal's office. The keys are on the desk. Maybe you could go and help him. Just give me time to get clear of this place.'

He sighed and nodded.

'Your horse is in the fourth stall, saddled and ready. I'm doin' this for Jessaka and maybe for Greg, too, seeing as how you could be a reincarnation of him. Now, you best get away.'

I murmured my thanks. I reached into my pocket, extracted the derringer and handed it to him. 'I hope you'll never have to use it,' I said.

It was Alfredo's roan that had been saddled — made ready, I guessed, by Jessaka. I wondered where she was now, but there was no time to find out. I hoped she wouldn't be in trouble for what she'd done, but I promised myself that one day I'd return for her — if I survived.

Within minutes I was astride the big horse and riding out of town, grateful that the hoofbeats were muffled by the street's dust.

Right then I figured I'd made a lucky escape, thanks to Jessaka and her father. But I had no idea of the awesome future that awaited me, nor that a military man, Sergeant McMahon, would be assigned the duty of capturing me and bringing me in dead or alive, as per the State Governor's instructions; dead being a cheaper option than a trial and hanging.

I rode long and hard into the afternoon, my intention being to get as far away as I could from Coltville. I kept clear of the main trails, passing through deep valleys and high bluffs, sometimes crossing hillsides cloaked in junipers and stands of pine. Whenever I reached a promontory I gazed back, straining my eyes for sign of pursuit, but I saw none and gradually my confidence grew.

We had paused several times at streams to quench our thirst, but by now I was both tired and hungry and the roan was weary and lathered. With evening approaching I found a sheltered copse and slipped from the saddle. I hobbled the roan and left her grazing contentedly. Finding a small cave I lay down inside, closed my eyes and was soon in dreamland.

I don't know how long I slept for, but I guessed it was a fair time. I was roused by a collard lizard running over my hand. Night had fallen and I could see the stars through the cave opening. There was a chill in the air. I got to my feet, feeling stiff. Hunger was gnawing at my belly like a crazy rat, but in the darkness I would stand no chance of catching any game.

I tried to work out where I was. I reckoned if I could get across the border into Arkansas I might find safety. If I kept going the way I was, I'd hit the road that led to the town of Barnford. With luck I might come upon an outlying farm or homestead and be able to find something to eat. A dozing chicken would be ideal.

Anyway, all I could do right now was press on. So I unhobbled the roan and mounted up. If I came to the road I'd follow along it. At least at this time of night there shouldn't be anybody around that would recognize me.

I struck the road sooner than I'd expected. Once on it, the going was easier and I prayed that soon I'd reach some human habitation.

I'd gone no more than a mile when, ahead of me, I saw the figures of two men standing upright in the moonlight at the roadside. I drew up, puzzled. They were standing so still beneath the branch of a great oak tree. It was as if they were apparitions deep in some mysterious conversation. But my guts reminded me of my pressing need. Maybe these men had food. I nudged the roan forward and we progressed cautiously.

The couple gave me no acknowledgement as I approached. Drawing close, I gasped with shock. Their feet were not touching the ground, but dangled some eighteen inches above it. The men were suspended by ropes looped over the branch above them, their necks stretched by strangling nooses, their arms bound behind their backs. There was no way of telling how long they'd been dead.

I felt sickened, but some inner compulsion had me taking a closer look. It was then I saw that there was something attached to the shirt-front of the victim on the left. It looked like the cover of a pasteboard shoe box. It had crude Roman characters scrawled upon it.

Straining my eyes in the moonlight, I could just make out the words:

BEWARE!
These are the first Victims to the Wrath of Outraged Citizens
More will follow
THE BALD KNOBBERS

Who the hell were 'the Bald Knobbers'?

My gaze swung up to the contorted faces of the corpses and my guts rumbled and a voice inside me cried out: But for the grace of God, go I!

7

The crazy notion came to me that my nose was dreaming. I'm sure it quivered as the most sumptuous aroma probed into my nostrils — an aroma of frying bacon. It was some twenty minutes after I'd said my farewells to the two fellows strung up by their necks, and here I was, faint with hunger, wondering if my senses were playing tricks with me.

As dawn fingered the eastern sky, I had quit the road, fearing that some pursuer might get sight of me, and taken to the trees. And now I drew up and convinced myself that what I was experiencing was real. Clearly somebody was cooking a breakfast close by. I debated whether I could take a risk and join this early-morning traveller and ask him to share his victuals with me. I could go in with gun drawn, if need be, and plunder his bacon, but I decided against this — at least in the initial introduction. Better to make a generous friend than a resentful enemy.

But then an alarming possibility struck me. This stranger might not be alone. There might be a group of killers ahead of me, the very devils who had lynched the two men. On the other hand they might have had nothing to do with it. I balanced the possibilities against each other, and my rumbling belly won the day. I would take a gamble.

I dismounted and rein-hitched the roan to a branch, then I boldly stepped forward, drawn by the redolence of sizzling bacon. No fragrance could have been more alluring.

'Hi there!' I called out, but I kept my hand close to the butt of my Colt .44, in case things turned sour.

A moment later, I stepped into a clearing and saw the alarmed faces of two men turned towards me. They were hunkered down close to a fire. One of them, a white-bearded, elderly man wearing spectacles, was dropping thick rashers of bacon into a frying pan. His younger partner had a rat's-tail moustache and cropped hair. His face was as thin as a knife-blade and mean-looking.

'Who in tarnation are you?' the older man exclaimed.

I gave them my friendliest smile. 'I'm sorry to disturb your breakfast, sir, but I'm so awful hungry and I wondered if you could spare me a bite to eat.'

That took them a moment to ponder on. I was the centre of hard scrutiny. Then the bearded one said, 'I asked you who you were. You didn't tell me.'

I cleared my throat and spoke in a meek voice. 'I've left home. You see, my ma died.' I wiped away a tear with the back of my hand. I went on: 'We lived over Branson way. There's nothin' left there for me, so I struck out on my own. But now I'm so hungry . . . '

The lean man had a hard eye. His gaze took in the gun holstered at my hip. Neither he nor his companion had any visible weapons. 'Could be a damned spy,' he commented. 'Maybe an Anti-Bald-Knobber!'

I guess my mouth sagged. I had no idea what he was talking about.

The older man seemed to be more conciliatory. 'Well, no matter who he is, I guess we can spare some grub, and maybe a drop of coffee.'

I murmured my thanks, and a moment later I was seated with them, wolfing back potatoes, a string of meaty bacon, and a chunk of corn bread. I had never tasted anything so delicious. I could just hear their questions above the crunch of my jaws.

'What's your name, son?'

I took a swallow, then answered straight: 'Billy Stark.'

Both men nodded. I was sure my name meant nothing to them.

'And where you headed?'

'Nowhere particular,' I said. 'I'm lookin' for work.'

For about five minutes we munched the food and then the thin man stood up. He was taller than I'd imagined.

'I need a pee,' he said, and he stepped to the trees at the side and fumbled with his clothing.

But he never peed. Instead, he spun on his heel and suddenly there was a gun in his hand. He must have had it in his pocket.

'Don't move or I'll plug you,' he warned in a snarling voice.

I felt sickened. I shot a despairing glance at the bespectacled man, hoping to see some compassion on his face. There was none, although he was grinning.

'You sure fell for that trick, Billy Stark!' he said. He leaned over and pulled my gun from its holster and tucked it into his belt, then he came to his feet and told me to do likewise. The other man kept me covered.

I cursed beneath my breath. The consoling fact was that I'd been fed.

'Where's your horse?' White-beard inquired.

I saw no point in lying. 'Tethered

down the slope.'

'We'll go fetch it,' he said, 'and don't try any tricks.'

He, too, now drew a pistol from his pocket and levelled it at me. I had a nasty feeling he'd use it if I attempted to escape. He and I scrambled down the slope to the roan. He unhitched him and led him back to the small campsite, making me walk ahead. Meanwhile his companion had cleared things up and stamped out the fire. He produced a rope and told me to put my hands behind my back. I glared at him but I complied and he bound my wrists together.

'Cap Buckthorn'll decide what to do with you,' he said.

This business wasn't going the way I'd intended, but right now there was nothing I could do about it.

Their horses were tethered nearby, and when they'd been retrieved, I was hoisted into my own saddle and my companions mounted up. We then set off, riding single file, me in the middle. The new day was taking hold, the sun already warm. I was sweating, not from the heat but from the anger that boiled inside me. If only I'd not been so damned hungry!

I wondered where they were taking me. And who was Cap Buckthorn? Why was he the one who would decide my fate?

We plodded on for a good half hour through pine forest. My arms ached from being tied. There was no conversation between us. We came to a trail and followed along it. I noticed housewife squirrels in the branches, gossiping at our passing, and envied them their freedom. The trail seemed well trodden, as if plenty of folks had passed along it. We eventually emerged on to flatter land and I saw a big, bald-topped hill looming ahead of us.

To my surprise, we started to climb it. The crest was barren of timber and underbrush. Later, I was to learn that the hill was known as Kelly's Bald. When we were halfway up, I could see that there was a small tent pitched on its summit. Around it, several men were standing, drinking from mugs. As we approached, our horses heaving at the incline, the burble of their voices became audible. With my arms secured, I had the utmost difficulty in remaining upright in the saddle.

The top of the hill was a flattened knob, almost desert-like, with no vegetation. We reached it and greetings were exchanged. I was dragged from the back of the roan none too gently. One man ducked out of the tent, and the others seemed to draw back in deference as he stepped through them to confront us. His gaze dwelt on me.

'Who have we here?' he said in a booming voice.

He was a giant, six and a half feet tall with no fat on his broad, thick-chested frame. He had a bushy, sandy-coloured beard and moustache and held himself like an army man. A general at least, I reckoned. Despite the heat, he was wearing a long, blue semi-military coat. I could feel his grey-blue eyes boring into me. He wasn't the only one staring. All the others were doing likewise.

My white-bearded captor spoke up. 'We found him snoopin' around, Cap Buckthorn. It was when we stopped for breakfast. He claimed he'd run away from home, but we figured he might be a spy.'

'A spy, eh?' Buckthorn said. 'Well, what do we do with spies?'

A response came from several men. 'We lynch 'em up, Cap!'

I could feel suspicion thickening the air about me. I felt desperate to defend myself.

'I'm not a spy!' I cried out.

'What are you doin' in these parts, then?' Buckthorn demanded.

'I left home because my ma died.' I had the distinct feeling I was pleading for my life. 'There was nothin' there for me. I figured to try and find work some-where. This mornin' I was so hungry. I smelled bacon cookin' and — '

'Get into the tent,' Buckthorn interrupted.

I walked through the group and ducked into the tent. Inside was a chair and a small table with some papers on it. Buckthorn followed me in, his sandy head brushing the roof. He lowered his huge frame into the chair.

'Sit down,' he ordered, indicating the floor. I did as instructed, finding it awkward with my arms still tied.

'You heard what we do with spies,' he said. 'Well, we do the same with liars. Now tell me the truth.'

I spent the next ten minutes going over my story again, though I didn't mention Alfredo or the attempt to lift the army payroll.

When I finished, Buckthorn took a long time thinking. The silence dragged on, broken only by the burble of voices from outside and the steady buzz of a bluebottle from inside. I felt a trickle of sweat run down the side of my face.

'Why should I believe you?' he asked.

I cast about in my mind for something intelligent to say. I could think of nothing. 'Because it's the truth,' I mumbled.

Again a lengthy pause while he debated my fate.

At last he spoke. 'Well, if you're misleadin' me in any way, you know what'll happen to you. I'm not a jokin' man. My task is to uphold righteousness and to bring wrongdoers to justice. Do you understand that?'

'Yes, sir,' I nodded.

'I need volunteers to help me in my work,' he went on. 'But I require absolute loyalty.' Then he asked, 'Do you believe in the Lord?'

Again I nodded. 'Most definitely.'

'Would you be willin' to help bring His word to this land?'

I didn't fancy the way things were headed, but on the other hand my options were limited. After a moment I said, 'Yes, sir. There's no other work for me right now. But I would need to have my arms untied.'

He didn't smile but uttered an understanding grunt. 'That will be no problem. Help me in my work, and the Lord's blessin' will be upon you. And

I'll arrange for you to earn your keep by doing farm duties in between our tasks. You'll have to take an oath of allegiance before you can join the Bald Knobbers. Do you understand? And if you break that oath, then you'll know what will happen to you.'

'Why are you called the Bald Knobbers?' I asked.

'Because we hold some of our meetin's here on the bald knob of this hill. From up here our guards can make sure we're not being spied on.'

Once more I nodded, little appreciating the awesome clan that I was committing myself to. I guessed I was not the first to be swayed by Buckthorn's towering presence.

8

Buckthorn called two of his men into the tent to act as witnesses. He picked up a knife from his table and, much to my relief, he leaned over me, so close I could smell him, and severed the rope binding my arms. As I stretched and rubbed them to restore the circulation, he produced a Bible and asked me to place my hand upon it.

'Repeat this after me,' he said. 'In the presence of God and these witnesses, I solemnly swear that I will never reveal any of the secrets of this order to a person not a member.'

I repeated his words. He read on, pausing for me to speak my part.

'I swear I will abide by the rules of this order and obey all orders of my superior officers. I will report all wrongdoin' that is made known to me, but not report anyone through personal enmity. Nor will I wilfully wrong or defraud a brother.

'Should I knowingly violate this oath, I will subject myself to the jurisdiction of members of this order, even if their decision should be to hang me by the neck until I am dead. So help me God.'

As the taking of the oath was concluded he told me that all the rules and arrangements were verbal and nothing was to be committed to paper. He also informed me that there was to be a meeting of all Bald Knobbers that very afternoon. It was the Sabbath.

He then consigned me to the care of one of the witnesses, a man called Lum Boothe. He was a grizzled and be-whiskered old-timer who told me he was a farmer. He seemed friendly enough and set me to work cleaning his rifle. I asked him if I could have my own gun returned. He went and asked Cap Buckthorn who gave his permission and my armoury was restored.

He clearly admired Nathaniel N. Buckthorn who, he told me, had been a prize fighter, a Pinkerton agent, a gun-slinger and an army scout. Now he was a ranch owner and Sunday school teacher.

I had no idea what my future was, but I figured that throwing in with this crowd was probably no bad thing. Here I was not recognized, and it was unlikely that the military or town marshal would come hunting for me amongst law-enforcing folk. If I did farm labour, I guessed I would be able to lay low. If nobody discovered my past, I should be safe enough. And maybe, if the chance came my way, I could run off. But then I recalled the oath I'd taken and the terrible fate Cap Buckthorn had promised for those who betrayed his trust. Like he'd said, he was not a joking man. He had taken a gamble in trusting me and it was best I played things straight, at least for a while.

At noon, I fed with the others, keeping as much to myself as I could. I felt I'd been accepted and was no longer treated with suspicion. Through the heat of the early afternoon, a steady flow of newcomers climbed the hill to Kelly's Bald. By three o'clock, when the meeting was scheduled to start, there must have been about sixty men assembled. I guessed they had all taken the oath. They appeared to come from all walks of life. Some wore their Sunday best, others the rough garb of farmers.

A small platform had been rigged up, obviously intended for the main speakers. When all were gathered, many of them sitting cross-legged on the ground, I stood alongside Lum Boothe with my ears pinned back.

Buckthorn, flanked by three of his officers, took to the platform, looking formidable on the raised dais. His orator's voice matched his appearance, strong and audible to every member of the hushed audience. He was better than any itinerant preacher I'd ever heard.

'My good men,' he commenced, 'I have brought you here today to confirm that our purpose is to deal quickly and effectively with border ruffians and rovin' gangs of thieves and outlaws.'

I quaked in my boots at that moment. Please God, I prayed, don't let him learn about my true past!

'Tubal and Frank Taylor,' he continued, 'have already had their necks stretched for their sins. There could be no other penalty severe enough for them. They had chopped out the tongues of Alex Kissee's prize cattle, causing them to starve to death. They had terrorized the citizens of Barnford by ridin' into town, discharging their guns. They had shot at Mrs Dickenson and blown off a finger. Now, thanks to us, their sinful days are finished.'

He paused, allowing his words to sink in. I recalled the two men I'd seen lynched. I wondered if they had been cut down yet, or were they still hanging there as a warning to other sinners — sinners like me?

Buckthorn went on: 'Law officers and juries have failed in their duties as American citizens, because criminals hold the county in a grip of fear. Honest, tax-payin' citizens have no protection from murderers, robbers, arsonists, horse thieves, cattle rustlers, petty crooks, rapists, loose women and free negroes.

'What will become of our sons and daughters? Our lives, property and liberty are at stake. Honest taxpayers' interests must be protected. I appeal to you as citizens of Taney County, Missouri, to agree with what we must do. That is why we have organized ourselves into a vigilante group to see that when crimes are committed they do not go unpunished. The alternative is to fold our arms and quietly submit.'

His final words came like a challenge. 'Good men, I wish to hear from you that we are all equally committed to this cause.'

An immediate and tremendous cheer erupted from the gathering. Fists were raised and some men chanted Buckthorn's name. There could be no doubt about their conviction.

That evening, as the gathering dispersed, the roan horse was returned to me, and I went home with Lum Boothe. He had agreed to employ me when I was not involved in Bald Knobber duties, whatever they were to be.

He farmed a big section of fertile bottomland and stocked his pastures with purebred cattle, blooded horses, dogs, sheep, hogs and mules. His house was solid-built and handsome.

Lum Boothe and his wife, a plump and friendly woman, took me into their home with immediate and unexpected kindness. Mrs Boothe asked me to call her Aunt Beth. It struck me that she wore the trousers in the household, often bending Lum to her will. They both seemed to take a liking to me, treating me as if I was one of the family.

I learned that they were in mourning. Their 17-year-old grandson, who had been living with them, had recently died of a heart seizure. The loss had left them deeply grieved. Maybe my advent had given them something to fill the gap.

They fed me well, inviting me to take

meals with them in their kitchen, and they provided me with ample sleeping straw in one of their barns and some clothing that had belonged to their grandson. Over the next days, I toiled conscientiously on the farm, helping the other farm hand, Fritz Hoffman, an elderly German. The work reminded me of my years at home.

Seeing that I was not a shirker, Lum Boothe said he would pay me a generous wage.

For two weeks I imagined that my fortunes had changed and that I might be able to shake off the shackles of my past. I wondered when my first assignment of Bald Knobber duty would arise and what form it would take.

I became aware that rumours were rife. Rustlers were at work in the county and Lum Boothe got so concerned that there were nights when we drove his cattle, sheep and horses deep into the woods for protection.

But if I'd thought that my past could remain locked away in a secluded corner of my head, I was in for a rude shock.

On the morning of my eighth day at the farm, Aunt Beth had asked me to clean the brass ornaments that decorated the parlour hearth. It was a warm day and the windows were open.

Kneeling, I was polishing when I heard voices coming from outside and a tremor of alarm went through me. I came to my feet and crept to the window. Through the net curtain I was afforded a view of the outside veranda. Lum and Beth Boothe were standing at the top of the steps, greeting a group of mounted bluecoat soldiers; my heart missed a beat right then.

Now the voices carried clearly to me. 'We're from Fort Sibley,' a man with three chevrons on his arm was saying. 'We're looking for a young outlaw who was part of a gang that tried to lift our army payroll. They walked into our trap and were all gunned down except for two of 'em. They got away and reached Coltville. One of 'em was wounded and died there. The other, a young fella, was arrested by the marshal and put in jail, but the devil escaped. He may be in these parts. We want to catch him so he can get the justice he deserves. He's a killer for sure. We wondered if you'd caught sight of him.'

I glanced around. Maybe I'd have to run and get out quick, but the room was like a trap. My exit would rapidly draw attention.

Outside, there seemed to be a stunned silence, then I heard Lum Boothe clear his throat. He said, 'Well, I'll be damned. I — '

He got no further because his wife interrupted him: 'We ain't seen any killers around here, but if we do, we'll sure let you know.'

In trepidation, I waited for Lum Boothe to contradict his wife. I listened, the blood pounding in my ears. All I heard was the sergeant's words.

'You best keep your eyes skinned. Remember he's dangerous.'

After a moment the clomp of hoofs

sounded as the soldiers turned their horses and rode off.

Utterly relieved, I slumped to the floor, my breath heaving. I'd come within a flea's hop of being captured and it wasn't a good feeling.

9

I returned to polishing the brass, working with a feverishness that was made more frantic by the nervous tension in me. I worried that the soldiers might return. I wondered if the Boothes would come to me and pound me with angry questions, but they didn't. I heard the sound of their voices coming from the kitchen, slightly raised in serious talk that I guessed centred around me, but strain my ears as I did, I couldn't discern their words. It was inconceivable that they hadn't realized I was the fugitive the military sought.

I knew my gun was hanging on a hook in the kitchen, alongside Lum's. I might need it sooner rather than later.

Aunt Beth had clearly saved me. I was sure she wasn't the lying sort, yet she'd done it, maybe because she'd developed an affection for me as my presence somehow compensated for the loss of her grandson. It made me feel humble.

As for Lum, I didn't know what he'd been in the process of saying to the soldiers, but he'd been cut off midstream. Perhaps, even now, he was angry with his wife for barging in. Perhaps his own feelings, fuelled by Buckthorn's threats to punish wrongdoers, were the opposite to hers. I knew he was a willing devotee of Buckthorn's ideals.

I felt apprehensive at the prospect of facing him again. And even if he did show me compassion, one slip of his tongue in the presence of Buckthorn or his sidekicks could spell a horrendous fate for me.

I finished the polishing and, gathering my nerve, I went to the kitchen, anxious to restore the comforting closeness of my gun. Lum wasn't there, but Aunt Beth was. She turned and gave me the warmest of smiles and asked me if I'd like a mug of coffee. I gratefully received it and she bustled about as if nothing of consequence had taken place.

I didn't see Lum for the rest of the day. Aunt Beth told me he was away on business. What business? I thought.

I worked hard, starting to dig a new well and keeping as close to the house as possible, remaining wary.

I knew that both law officers and military would be anxious to track me down. Also, other Bald Knobbers might have been approached by the military and thus put two and two together, but I tried to push the thought from my head.

When Lum came back in the evening, he was serious-faced, but he made no mention of the army visit. Instead, he told me that Bald Knobbers were to meet on Bender's Bridge at dusk on the following day. There was work to be done.

I wondered if I was being lured into a trap where my identity would be revealed, but I dismissed the thought.

Lum was too decent a man to fall so low — I hoped.

That night I couldn't sleep. Ghastly visions of being captured churned inside my head. But then as I tossed and turned, an image of Jessaka probed into my thoughts. She looked so clean and pretty and smiling that she replaced images of my grim prospects. I knew it was crazy. I'd only met her for the briefest moment, yet something had passed between us, something that was precious and wonderful, telling me that she felt the same about me as I did about her.

The next day passed uneventfully and, after an early supper, Lum and I saddled up and set out for the appointed meeting place. He was unusually quiet and my mind was filled with fearful suspicions.

By the time we had reached the remote Bender's Bridge, darkness had flooded in and the moon was obscured by cloud. The others, about a dozen men, were already there, including

Nathaniel Buckthorn. We were greeted with quick informality, and this somewhat eased my concerns of a trap. It seemed there were bigger fish to fry.

Buckthorn launched into one of his sermon-like addresses, his face indiscernible in the gloom. 'My good men, tonight we must undertake a task of utmost importance. The couple calling themselves Clayman have been livin' in sin, fornicatin', with their union unblessed by God. This is a blight on our community and must not be allowed. Two weeks ago switches were placed outside their cabin, with a warning that the sinners were to leave the county. But they have defied us and remained. Tonight they must pay the penalty. The switches will be applied.'

There was a general murmur of approval in the group.

Buckthorn went on: 'Turn your coats inside out and put the sacks over your heads. Nobody must be able to prove who we are.'

Everybody removed their coats, me

included, turning them wrong side out, and replaced them. I noticed that several of my confederates were holding switches. One man passed round what appeared to be old flour sacks with two slits cut for the eyes. When I slipped mine over my head, I found that these holes were too low and I hoisted the sack back for clearer vision. I assumed that the previous wearer had had a long forehead. Everybody was now unrecognizable. I couldn't even identify Lum Boothe.

We seemed to be acting like outlaws, up to no good, not that I could boast an unblemished past. Even so, I had a queasy feeling in my stomach. But now, all I could do was follow along with the others.

Soon we were galloping through the night, moving like phantoms, and fifteen minutes later we drew rein before a small cabin. It was set alone on a little hillock in an oak forest, and lights showed through its curtained windows.

Buckthorn, forever the leader, nudged

his horse forward, cupped his hands to his mouth and sent his voice booming.

'Come outside, you Claymans, and face the punishment you deserve!'

We waited. There was no response, then the inside lamps were snuffed out, plunging the place into complete darkness.

Buckthorn grunted with impatience and then repeated his command. This time there was a reaction. A shot cracked out and the Bald Knobber next to me emitted an oath and clutched his shoulder, his horse prancing nervously. We all backed off slightly, seeking cover in the undergrowth, and dismounted.

'Let's teach them a lesson,' Buckthorn called, drawing his two pistols. Everybody snatched out their weapons, me included, though I had no intention of killing anybody. I determined to aim off.

Soon a barrage of bullets was splintering the cabin's logs and smashing the glass in the windows. But when there was a pause in our first burst, retaliation came in the form of fire from

93

a powerful repeating rifle — a Springfield, I guessed. The shots went wide but had us ducking our heads.

A moment later, the Bald Knobbers resumed their assault. I blazed away. Nobody seemed to notice the futile direction of my aim. The noise was deafening as a mass of lead slammed into the abode's timbers. Those inside were no doubt crouched down, away from the windows, momentarily sheltered.

I asked myself what the hell I was doing in this situation. I pitied the couple who had done nothing worse than surrender to their love for each other. It occurred to me that my own mother and Alfredo had lived for a time in similar circumstances. Thank God the Bald Knobbers had never cottoned on to them.

Buckthorn's voice cut through the racket, calling for us to cease fire. The blast of shots subsided, but the singing in my ears continued. Even so, I heard his next words.

'We're wastin' our ammunition. We

gotta get 'em out. We'll try somethin' different. Joe . . . you go around the back of the place. There are no doors or windows there. Toss a burnin' brand onto the roof.'

'With pleasure, Cap.' Joe disappeared into the darkness.

We waited in silence as the minutes ticked past. No more bullets came our way. Maybe the couple had exhausted their supply and were unable to offer further resistance. But now the die was cast because fire pierced the gloom, shooting up from the cabin's roof. It didn't take long before flame was spreading, crackling fiercely, sending sparks and smoke into the night sky. With the absence of rain for some weeks, the timbers were dry and before long they were encompassed by a greedy blaze.

While we watched, I heard Buck-thorn growl, 'Come out, you sinners!'

As if heaven answered his plea, the scampering couple emerged through the cabin's doorway. The woman was screaming. The man paused to beat out flames from her clothing.

'Grab 'em, boys,' Buckthorn cried. 'Tie 'em up!'

I trailed at the rear as our group charged forward and seized the hapless pair. The woman continued to scream but otherwise they made no effort to defend themselves. Maybe the man didn't struggle because he was fearful of what would happen to the woman. They were outnumbered and beaten. There was no alternative but to surrender to their fate.

I was not involved. The too-big flour bag had flopped over my eyes and I strove to pull it back. When I succeeded, I was standing behind the others as they grouped around their victims and my view was hampered. Not that I would have welcomed the sight.

What followed made me physically sick. I pulled up my wretched mask and vomited my supper into the dirt.

It was a nightmare. It was horrendous. It was like a tableau, etched there in the bright light of the blazing cabin. Clayman had had his shirt torn off and was bare buff. The woman's dress had been ripped from her shoulders. Both their pale backs were exposed. They stood close together, rope binding them to the trunk of a big oak tree, faces pushed against the bark. Around them circled the half dozen hooded men who had hickory withes, shouting in vengeful cries. As each tormentor came abreast of them, he lashed out with his withe, striking each back with all his might. On and on the thrashing went. It seemed it would never stop.

At first, man and woman screamed as the withes bit home, turning ugly red wields into wounds from which blood spurted. After a while, the woman stopped screaming and slumped down, held up only by the bonds. I wondered if she was dead, or had she merely fainted? The man grew silent, remaining upright, his body shuddering at each blow.

When those administering the punishment were exhausted, they thrust their withes towards the four of us who had not taken part. 'Your turn to show 'em!' somebody yelled out, and I knew that Buckthorn's merciless eye was upon us. I felt a withe pushed into my hand, saw the gore and pieces of flesh that showed on it. Somehow, I was forced forward with the others. I felt in a daze as we circled, striking the naked backs. I strove to hold back at the last moment, praying that my softened blows inflicted no agony and would go un-noted by my companions. I felt a sense of cowardliness that I had never experienced before.

When it was over we stood back, the others panting with exertion, and Buckthorn commanded that they be cut loose. When this was done, they both fell like limp, blood-covered dolls to the ground.

Buckthorn, looking immense in the flame light, stood over the man. He prodded him roughly with his boot until he stirred.

'Get out of this county,' he cried. 'If you and your harlot are not gone by tomorrow night, we'll lynch you properly!' And with that, he turned and strutted to where the horses were tethered. The others followed.

I was awestruck with the nightmare of it all. I just stood there gazing at what we'd done — the blazing cabin, now reduced to a blackened hulk, the poor wretches who had suffered so much. It was then that the man raised his head and twisted towards me, his features contorted with agony. And I died a small death.

It was my pa!

10

I should have gone to my father, snatched off my mask, done what I could for him. But I did not. All I could manage was to turn tail and run, as if escape from the scene would somehow bring me awake from a terrible nightmare.

I was in mental turmoil as I caught up with the others and hauled myself into the roan's saddle. Your own father, a voice was screaming inside my head, your own father, and you whipped him! And all the time I was haunted by the uncertainty of what would happen to him. Could he and his woman companion recover from what they'd suffered? Would they be able to leave the county, or would they remain and fall victim to Buckthorn's terrible threat of lynching?

I detested the Bald Knobbers then, and everything, everybody associated with them, including myself.

I had no memory of the return ride, of the others going their separate ways. All I recall were the awful images that haunted me: of flames dancing high, of masked figures, of two naked backs lacerated to a bloody pulp. If there is a hell to which the wicked go, it will be like that.

Lum Boothe and I travelled back and there were no words between us. I wondered if he was as stunned and shocked as I was, but I'm sure he wasn't. Despite his sometime façade of easy-going affability, of submissiveness towards his wife, he must have been as bigoted and merciless as the others. There were two things that remained a mystery. The first was why he had never betrayed me to the army or his compatriots. He must have known, or had suspicions, about me. The second was whether Aunt Beth was aware of his evil night-time missions. I didn't have the answers.

As for Nathaniel Buckthorn, I hated

him and the hypocrisy of his so-called Christianity. It cut into me with the sharpness of a knife.

But by next morning, life had returned to its normal domesticity. At least on the surface. I couldn't eat breakfast because I felt sick. I yearned to ride to the cabin and discover what had happened after our departure — but I could not.

Lum Boothe was out early, attending to his chores on the farm and so was I, though I kept away from him. I worked with Fritz Hoffman, the German hand, slaughtering and butchering a hog. In the afternoon, we continued to work on the new well.

During the day, I was aware that riders came to the farm. I suspected that they brought messages. I felt uneasy as to what those messages were.

Come evening, Lum Boothe sought me out as I was putting away spades in the barn. My insides grew tight as he approached but he gave me a smile.

'Billy' he said, 'there's another Bald

Knobbers job for us.' He paused, thumbing baccy down in his pipe.

'You mean to go to the Clayman place and see if they've gone?' I asked.

He shook his head. 'No, Nathaniel'll see to that. This is a job next Friday. I don't know exactly what it is but — '

Revulsion rose in my throat like bile. I stammered out: 'I'm n-not goin' to do it!'

His jaw sagged, his face turning mean.

'You are goin',' he snapped at me. 'You're a Bald Knobber, just like the rest of us. You took the oath to obey at all times, remember?'

I was taken aback by his changed manner. I didn't answer and after a second he turned on his heel and stomped from the barn.

More restless nights, and two more days passed, during which I yearned for news, even some gossip about the burning out of the Claymans' cabin but none came and my impatience, my concern for my father, increased until I could stand it no longer.

In my turmoil, I reached a decision. I confronted Lum and asked him if I could have the afternoon off, as I had some important business to attend to.

He gave me a bemused look. 'If you leave here,' he said, 'you'll hightail it and never come back. But I can tell you, Buckthorn or his associates'll come after you, hunt you down like a runaway black. He'll have you strung up the same as he did the Taylors. You won't stand a chance.'

His words had ended as a tirade. When he stopped he stood looking at me, seeing what effect the threat had.

I forced myself to be calm. 'I'll be back before sundown,' I said. 'I promise.'

He hesitated, then nodded. 'Don't let me down,' he said.

So it was that I presently saddled the roan and set out for the Claymans' cabin — or what was left of it. As I rode, the forbidding thought arose in me that my father and the woman might still have refused to move out, or indeed might have been too injured to travel. Would I find them lynched from a tree, flies gathering on their bodies, Buckthorn's final threat fulfilled? Anxiety had me heeling the roan for greater speed.

I knew I was nearing the place before I reached it. Smoke and ash still tainted the air. I approached and scanned the surrounding trees, fearful that I would encounter dangling bodies or even a noosed rope hanging down, but I saw nothing. However, what was left of the homestead was there to taunt me.

Not a timber remained unblackened. The roof, walls and supports had caved in. There was still a smouldering amid the ruin of it all, a smudge of redness here and there, and I felt the heat of it on my face. Nothing was left of the furnishing and other contents. Here, had once been a simple home.

I sat there, engulfed with a mixture of sadness and bitterness. At last I concluded that there wasn't anything to be gained by remaining at this place apart from strengthening the gruesome memories that moiled in my head. At least I now felt assured that my father was gone, that he had conceded to Buckthorn's demands. I just prayed that he, and his woman, would recover from their awful injuries.

So it was that I turned the roan and rode off, at first aimlessly. I had vague ideas of one day seeking my father and making some sort of peace with him, if not now, then later, but just how I was going to do this I couldn't imagine. Of course, everything depended on whether I survived or not.

Ten minutes later, I came upon a cabin, similar to the Claymans', set on a hill slope from which the trees had been cleared. There was an old man with a great long beard sitting on the veranda. At first, as I approached, he appeared to be asleep, but a snort from my horse caused him to raise his head.

'Howdy,' I cried out.

He didn't answer but bit off a plug of

baccy and chewed away. I noticed that there was a rifle leaning against the wall next to him.

'I wondered,' I said, 'if you knew what happened to the Claymans.'

'Claymans!' He at last found his voice. 'Why, what's it to you?'

'I'm related,' I said.

He grunted contemptuously and his jaw worked his baccy. 'Related?' he questioned. 'What d'you mean related?'

I felt a desire to be truthful. 'I'm his son,' I said.

'Well,' he said, 'maybe you know he and his woman got worked over the other night and his place was burned down. The devils what did it deserve to rot in hell.'

I nodded and swallowed hard.

'You knew about it?' he asked.

I hesitated, then said, 'I've just seen what's left of the place.'

He went on. 'Well, when I see the smoke, I got over there as quick as I could. That was three or four nights ago. But I was too late to do anythin'.

They was sure in a bad way, but Dan Clayman swore he was gonna pull out, mainly for his woman's sake.' He gave his bony shoulders a helpless shrug and repeated, 'Nothin' I could do.'

'Did they say where they were headin'?' I asked.

He scratched his head, stirring up his memory. 'Yup, I recall. He mentioned his woman had relatives over in Arkansas. Talked about a place called Benton. They're probably there by now, that's if they managed the journey.'

I nodded my gratitude. I somehow felt I'd won a small victory, though looking back, it didn't seem I had much to celebrate.

The old man softened his attitude. He told his life story, and talked about his wife who'd dropped dead one day last year. 'Glad to see the back of the old biddy,' he admitted.

I couldn't concentrate on his words. My mind was too full of my father. As soon as it seemed right, I took my leave, thanking the old man again.

I guess it was then that I faced a kind of Rubicon. I confess that I considered taking the action that Lum had suspected I would take, and attempt to ride away and leave the whole ghastly Bald Knobber mess behind me. I could try and find my father. Of course, there was the chance he might not welcome me. Maybe he'd blotted me from his memory years ago.

And I had thoughts of Buckthorn's wrath. I recalled how the Taylors had looked hanging by their necks. Also, I had taken the oath on a Bible and made a promise to Lum Boothe.

Finally there was Aunt Beth. No matter what sins Lum committed, she was a warm-hearted woman who had shown me every kindness. Indeed, in turning away the soldiers she had probably saved my life. I couldn't just walk out on her without a word of appreciation.

Whether it was having given my word, or fears of Buckthorn's vengeance, or my feelings for Aunt Beth that swayed me along the path I took, I wasn't sure, but I suspected the latter.

I heeled the roan towards the Boothes' farm. I would be back before sundown.

11

If Lum Boothe was surprised to see me return, he didn't show it. That night I slept soundly and without dreams. Apart from its overwhelming weariness, I guess my brain was tired of being pounded with questions it couldn't answer. Nor, it seemed, did it contemplate mountains I was yet to climb. But when I rose, shortly after dawn, all my concerns returned.

After breakfast, Lum Boothe sent Fritz Hoffman and me into the woods to collect hickory branches. More withes were needed. Similar to the ones used to punish my father. The recollection made me shudder, but now I went about my task, hoping that what I collected would not be used for such evil purposes.

Presently old Fritz enlightened me, and I figured he knew plenty about the Bald Knobbers, though he was not one himself. He told me that Buckthorn had a list of all the families 'living in sin', as well as women of loose morals, men paying too much attention to their neighbours' wives and petty criminals generally. Buckthorn was determined to drive them from the county.

The practice was that, during darkness, the Bald Knobbers would approach the home of the sinners, and leave a hickory withe outside. This was known as a warning that such sinners should immediately leave. If they failed to comply, the night-riders would return and inflict their terrible whippings. In severe cases, lynching was possible. Sinners tended to get out while they had the chance.

After we returned, laden, from the woods, Fritz set to work, binding switches into suitable bundles. Lum Boothe had another duty for me. He wanted me to accompany him into Coltville to help him collect supplies.

I tried to conceal my apprehension. If I happened to come face to face with Doc Wilmer, the sheriff, or certain deputies, I would be in serious trouble. But then the thought that I might see Jessaka lifted my spirits. In any event, I set out with Lum in the buckboard wagon.

The church clock was striking noon as we reached town. Lum may have wondered why I kept my hat pulled low, but he didn't comment. We went directly to the main mercantile store and hitched the wagon so that our horse had easy access to the water trough. As we went in, Lum pulled out the shopping list that Aunt Beth had prepared.

While he placed his order, I purchased a handsome knife and sheath, which I attached to my belt.

When we had everything we needed, we loaded the supplies onto the wagon. It was a bright day and I stayed back in the shadow of the stoop as best I could, keeping a steady watch on the folks passing up and down the street, but I saw nobody I recognized. My mind turned to Jessaka. The hostelry was only a stone's throw away and I yearned to speak with her, to express my gratitude, or even just catch a glimpse of her. However, I was given no chance; Lum was anxious to get back. So we climbed aboard the wagon, he flicked the reins and we were on our way.

We little dreamed of what awaited us.

It was an hour later and despite the constant roar of the springboard's wheels, I had lapsed into a doze. The trail was flanked by a river on the left; to the right the land rose to a line of bluffs. That was when the shot sounded, a deadly crack that sliced through the wagon's racket. I was awake in an instant, realizing, horrified, that Lum had slumped over on the seat and that blood was pumping from his shoulder. The reins had slipped from his grasp.

The horse was panicked and we were suddenly careering forward, bouncing so roughly that Lum started to topple from his seat. I made a frantic grab for him but I wasn't quick enough and he fell from the wagon and I lost sight of him.

Balancing desperately, I grappled to retrieve the reins, but we pounded on for some distance and, as I forced back the brake, we slewed off the trail over a bank and into the brush. Only then did we come to a halt. The horse had fallen and was thrashing his legs.

Shakily, I climbed down. I scrambled back onto the trail and gazed over the way we'd come. I saw Lum's body lying motionless about fifty yards off. I cursed. I glanced at the bluffs. I could see no sign of the marksman, but it was clearly from the bluffs that he'd fired. He was most likely still there, waiting to get another shot in.

Who the hell was he?

I pondered on what I should do. Lum might already be dead and if I returned to him, I'd be as exposed as a fly on a drum top. On the other hand our assailant might have withdrawn, and there was another possibility: maybe Lum was still alive. I decided I had to find out.

I drew my gun and hurried towards him. At first, I kept to the cover of the trailside brush, but I was finally obliged to take to open ground. I went, instinctively ducking my head, fearing the crack of a gun at any moment.

Unscathed, I reached Lum. Flies were already swarming around his bloody shoulder. He was sprawled on his back. I dropped to my knees beside him. I saw his nostrils flaring and knew he was breathing, but falteringly. His eyes were closed. I called his name. His eyelids flickered and he groaned.

I glanced up at the bluffs and saw no movement. Please God, I thought, may the gunman have gone.

My attention swung back to Lum. Now I saw that his eyes were open.

'We've got to move you,' I gasped, and somehow he managed to nod.

He attempted to rise, but couldn't make it. I slid my hands beneath his armpits, felt the wetness of his blood. He cried out with pain as I hauled him onto his feet. He would have fallen back had I not supported him. I was afraid he might have broken his back when he'd come off the wagon, but as he moved his limbs I reckoned that was not the case. He wasn't a heavy man and for this I was thankful. I half carried him to the side of the trail and we slumped down into the cover of the brush.

'Who fired at you?' I asked.

It was an effort for him to speak, but his lips moved and his response was only just audible. 'Damned Anti-Bald-Knobbers!'

This didn't make much sense to me, but I saw that further explanation would be too much for him.

I wondered what the condition of the horse and wagon was. I decided I would have to find out. Giving an assurance I would return, I left Lum and scrambled away.

To my relief I found that the horse was back on his feet and appeared to be uninjured. I climbed onto the box seat and after minutes of extreme effort by both animal and myself, managed to get the wagon back onto the trail. I then drove to where I had left Lum. To my surprise, he was standing up. He was clutching his shoulder, his face twisted with pain, but with my help, he climbed onto the seat.

He was losing a lot of blood as we covered the remaining miles back to the farm, wincing at every bump in the trail, but somehow we made it.

When we pulled into the yard, Aunt Beth and Fritz were there to meet us, their faces taut with alarm as they saw Lum's condition. Soon, we were supporting him into the house, resting him down on his bed. It was then that he raised himself, placed his hand on my arm and murmured, 'Thanks, Billy.'

His wife fetched a bowl of water and bandages. While she went to work, bathing the wound, Fritz said, 'I'll ride to town, fetch the doctor.'

Aunt Beth nodded and he turned and left us.

Concern clawed at my vitals. The doctor from town — Wilmer . . . he who had known I was fleeing from the law and had lured me into a trap.

12

Presently, when Aunt Beth hurried away to get some more bandages, Lum Boothe beckoned me to him. He was very weak and the thought was in me that he might not pull through. But he gripped my sleeve and drew me close.

'Billy,' he whispered, 'I promised we would ride with the Bald Knobbers tomorrow night. I'm . . . I'm pretty sure I'm not goin' to be fit enough.' He paused, summoning up his strength, then he said, 'But you must go. They're meetin' at the same place, same time. We can't let Nathaniel down. Promise me you'll go.'

I guess seeing him so poorly, maybe at death's door, it seemed that refusing him anything would be downright churlish. He was gazing at me intently, desperate for my answer. I knew I could be letting myself in for something I might deeply regret, but right then I didn't have it in me to refuse him.

'I promise,' I said, and he rested back, emitting a relieved sigh. He closed his eyes.

Lum Boothe could seem downright decent at times, but when he put the Bald Knobber mask over his head, the other side of his character came to the fore and he was driven by intolerant principles.

For reasons I'll never be able to explain, I desperately wanted him to survive.

After Aunt Beth returned with more bandages, I unloaded the supplies from the wagon, then I unhitched the horse and set him to graze.

My thoughts swung to my own predicament. Most likely, and within a few hours, Fritz would bring Doc Wilmer back to the farm. This could spell disaster for me. I would have to make myself scarce. Come early evening, I took my leave of Aunt Beth and retired to my corner on the upper floor of the barn. Through a hole in the planking, I had a good view of the yard.

The hours dragged by without the arrival of Fritz and the doctor. I wondered if the medical man was out of town, or maybe he had refused to come. This would be good news for me, but not for Lum's chances of survival. Night settled in with a moon as bright as a silver dollar. At last I heard the stomp of hoofs from the yard. Through the hole, I glimpsed Fritz and the unmistakable figure of Doc Wilmer dismounting. Aunt Beth greeted them and ushered them inside.

I slumped back onto my bed, wishing I was a thousand miles away. The night was warm and I was sweating and I could do nothing but wait. I must have dozed off because I recall waking up and hearing voices in the yard. When I spied out, I saw Wilmer mount up and ride away.

Later, when I went down to the house, I found Aunt Beth fussing over Lum. The doctor, she said, had confirmed that the bullet had passed through, entering his back and exiting close to his heart. The loss of blood had been massive.

'Lum was delirious,' she explained. 'He rambled on about how his young man saved him. The doc wanted to know all about you. He seemed so interested.' She paused, her fingers touching her lips in sudden concern. 'Maybe I shouldn't have told him.'

I didn't say anything, but my spirits had sunk to my boots.

She went on: 'After he dosed Lum with opiates to ease the pain and make him sleep, he said he'd come back first thing in the mornin'.'

It was a bitter pill to swallow. When Wilmer returned, he'd probably bring the marshal and a posse with him. I was going to have to get out fast and be well clear of the farm by daybreak.

Aunt Beth looked puzzled as I stepped forward and kissed her cheek. Once, she'd saved me from capture. Now, unwittingly, she had plunged me into new jeopardy, but I could not hold it against her and my memories of her would always be sweet.

She sensed I was leaving and prepared bread, pork and a pie for me to take. I thanked her for all her kindness. I also asked her to tell Lum that I would keep the promise I had given him for the following evening. Then, with a heavy heart, I left her, recovered the roan from the grazing corral and saddled him.

When I rode out across the moonlit meadow, I knew that I had to put miles between me and this place which had been a haven of safety but no longer was.

I spent the next day hiding out in a river gulley, my only company, apart from the roan, the birds, squirrels and a red fox, which blundered into my space, then back-tracked frantically.

Come evening, I set off for the meeting point at Bender's Bridge. I went, trying to ignore the fear that news of my identity might have leaked to the Bald Knobbers. As I reached the bridge, a voice challenged me from the shadows:

'Who goes there?'

Lum had once told me of the passwords I must use if I ever came alone.

'Bell,' I responded.

'Whose bell?'

'My bell.'

I rode forward and suddenly other men appeared about me and I was greeted with the usual informality. I glanced around. I counted eight Bald Knobbers present, mostly different from those involved in the last job. Nathaniel Buckthorn was not there.

An intense conversation was taking place. One man claimed he had found some of his stock lying dead on the range; another said his barn had been set on fire; three more stated that they had been shot at as they ploughed their fields. They all seemed to have heard that Lum Boothe had been shot.

A man called Ben Walker said, 'Buckthorn knows about it. He says it's the Anti-Bald-Knobbers responsible.'

Another man called out, 'I reckon we

should swap work. Instead of ploughing alone, five or six of us should work together and maybe patrol the fields, armed with rifles.'

Everybody present grunted agreement.

But now focus swung to the work due to be done tonight. Ben Walker, who seemed to be leading the group, was positively hyped up, insane with the craving for revenge against an individual called Albert Wolfskin. Wolfskin, apparently, was a notorious horse thief. He had been brought to court but acquitted because he had cohorts on the jury. After the trial, Wolfskin had not mended his ways. In fact Ben Walker claimed that Wolfskin had recently stolen horses from him, herded them into Arkansas and sold them. The object of tonight's mission was to ensure, Walker vowed, that Wolfskin would never commit crime again. I knew what that meant and I felt sick about it.

For the first time I noticed that among the group was a church minister. He knelt and prayed aloud that the Lord would be with us tonight as we ventured forth to punish sinners. The others bowed their heads. I guess they all professed to be religious.

Flour sacks were passed around. We donned these and turned our coats inside out as was the custom. Walker screamed, 'Let's go get 'im, boys!' and our little cavalcade galloped into the moonlit night. Walker led us at a feverish pace. To me, they seemed like a pack of wolves burning with blood lust, and I was carried along with them in their flood of hatred.

It was half an hour later that we pulled up in front of Wolfskin's lonely cabin. It was in complete darkness, but at the side I saw a number of horses in a corral. Walker dismounted and drew his two pistols. He marched up to the door of the place and hammered it with the butt of one of his guns. He yelled, 'Open up, Wolfskin. We need to talk to you!'

There was a long pause, then a light showed in the window and a man's voice called, 'Who's there?'

'We want a word with you,' Walker replied.

As we sat on our horses watching, the man next to me sniggered and murmured, 'Sure do.'

Two other Bald Knobbers dismounted and tossed a rope over the extended limb of a big oak tree, some fifteen feet above them, only succeeding in their aim after two attempts. I glimpsed the waiting noose dangling down.

Suddenly the door of the cabin rattled open and a man appeared, silhouetted in the lamplight. 'What the hell . . . ?' he gasped out.

Walker had both his guns pointed at him. 'Albert Wolfskin, we've come so you can pay your debt, you damned horse thief.'

The man hesitated, noisily sucking air into his lungs, his voice coming in a high-pitched terrified gush. 'I'm not Albert. I'm his brother. I came here to talk some sense into him, to say give up breaking the law. But he's away . . . I ain't seen him.'

Walker unleashed an impatient growl. 'You're a goddamned liar, Albert Wolfskin, but your lies don't fool us!' He swung towards his followers. We'd all dismounted.

'Grab 'im, boys,' Walker hollered.

I watched, sickened, and remained in the rear as the mob surged forward. Wolfskin turned back, tried to escape into the cabin, but he stood no chance. He was seized and dragged out. And all the time he was yelling, 'Not Albert. I'm his brother.'

Some of the Bald Knobbers started chanting, 'Liar! Liar!' Nobody believed him, except maybe me.

The whole scene merged into a horrific nightmare. He was screaming and struggling as his hands were fastened behind him. The noose was fitted over his head and he was forced up onto the back of a nervously prancing horse, then the rope was drawn taut and tied down.

Walker, who had been holding the horse, now released it, uttering a yell. The animal needed no further invitation but galloped off, leaving the gurgling Wolfskin twisting to and fro, his legs kicking as he fought, choking, against encroaching oblivion.

Something approaching a cheer rippled through the Bald Knobbers. One man set off to recover the run-off horse, whilst the others climbed into their saddles and, the grisly deed done, they spurred away into the darkness.

We were soon passing through scrub oak. I was at the rear. I had slowed, a desperate plan forming in my mind. Nobody heeded me as I reined in and turned the roan back. A moment later I had returned to the site of the lynching and jumped from the saddle. Wolfskin was still twitching.

I went round to the back of the oak, drew my knife and slashed the knotted rope. I heard the thump as he dropped to the ground. I rushed to him, knelt down and cut the rope binding his arms. To my surprise, his eyes were open, his mouth yawning wide as breath fought its way in and out of his tortured throat.

'Get away from here,' I shouted into his ear. 'Get away and don't come near this place again!'

I swear his head gave the faintest of nods.

I left him then. As I spurred back the way I'd come, the enormity of what I'd done weighed upon me. If Walker, or Buckthorn, discovered my actions, I would be the next one for lynching.

I didn't know whether the man I'd cut down was Albert Wolfskin or his brother, but I hoped he was the latter. No man deserved a lynching if any doubts existed. But Ben Walker had had no doubts. I suspected that neither he, nor any of the others, had ever come face to face with Albert Wolfskin and had only known him by reputation. And maybe I would never learn the true identity of the man I'd cut down.

I determined to catch up with the others as quickly as possible. I urged the roan forward. Suddenly a horseman loomed out of the darkness in front of me and blocked the path. I pulled up, trepidation cutting through me. I saw he was wearing a Bald Knobber mask. For a moment I wondered if he was returning to the lynched man, maybe to retrieve his rope. Anxious to prevent him from proceeding further, I swung the roan side-on, barring his way. He seemed not to notice.

'Wondered where you got to,' he said. 'Ben Walker sent me back to find you.'

I blurted out the first thing that entered my head. 'Horse picked up a stone. I stopped to prize it out.'

He didn't respond immediately. He pondered over my explanation. At last he said, 'OK.' He turned his horse and we went on at a brisk trot and presently caught up with the others.

Before we disbanded at Bender's Bridge, Walker turned to me and said, 'Better not forget the meetin' at Bagel's Spring tomorrow night. You got to stand in for Lum now.'

'I'll be there,' I said, but I wasn't sure I would be.

13

I returned to my hiding place in the river gulley and slept away what was left of the night. I dreamed of making love with Jessaka, but then Alfredo somehow stepped into the dream and I saw his face, contorted with agony. When I awoke, shaken, the sun had risen and my stomach was rumbling. I carried out a cautious hunt in the woods and shot a squirrel, which I roasted over a small fire. I was so desperate to satisfy my hunger, that it was still half raw when I ate it.

I wondered if Lum had survived, and also Wolfskin. Thoughts of Wolfskin brought back my fears. Supposing the Bald Knobbers discovered what I had done? But still I didn't regret it. I must admit I was scared, dead scared, but somehow I felt that my safest option was to stay with the vigilantes and keep the appointment at the meeting, rather than take my chances alone. Twice, during the afternoon, I changed my mind; twice I reverted back to my original intent.

As I approached Bagel's Spring that night, I was challenged and spoke the passwords before I was allowed in. Bagel's Spring was a large hollow through which the spring flowed, bordered by trees. It was a remote and lonely place. My arrival stirred up no more interest than normal. There were about a dozen men present, including Buckthorn. I had realized that the practice of the Bald Knobbers was to operate in small hand-picked groups. Tonight, it seemed that the gathering was made up of the clan's hierarchy. I knew I was here to represent Lum Boothe. Somebody inquired after him. Obviously word had got around, which it did by mysterious means among the Bald Knobbers. I told them he was holding his own. I hoped I was right. They appeared unaware that I had left the farm.

Above the burble of conversation, I heard Buckthorn say, 'I took no pleasure in killing Coggburn, but he deserved nothing better.'

I had no idea who Coggburn was.

Buckthorn went on, 'Andrew Coggburn and his brothers have been terrible trouble-makers. They've openly criticized the Bald Knobbers. They disrupted my Sunday school teaching. They even bragged they'd kill me. Last Sunday I came face to face with Coggburn. I could see he intended to carry out his threat because he reached for his gun. He must have forgotten I was once a gun-slinger. In self-defence, I drew my own gun and shot him.'

Buckthorn's explanation, it seemed, came from his heart and was met with all-round approval.

'There was only one witness to the killing,' Buckthorn went on, 'and that was Coggburn's sidekick, Sam Snapp, who has sworn blind to the sheriff that I went for my gun first, and that after I'd killed Coggburn I placed his gun in his hand to make it look like he was gunning for me.'

His words brought a growl of indignation from those listening. One thing nobody had ever done before was to accuse Buckthorn of being a liar.

A man called Joe McGill now spoke up. 'Nathaniel, in view of the falsehoods that Snapp is spreading, I guess he needs takin' care of.'

Buckthorn nodded, but he branched out on a different tangent. 'We've got a fight on our hands. We all know that Coggburn and others set up the group calling themselves the Anti-Bald-Knobbers, and they are goin' out of their way to take shots at us, destroy our crops, kill our hogs. Now I've heard that some of them are vowin' to shoot us on sight. We've got to crush them, by force if necessary. We must not let them interfere with our good work.'

Once again his support came thick and fast. I went along with the others as I didn't want to stand out.

Buckthorn went on: 'Now we'll return to the question of Snapp. We can't afford to let him spread his lies.

He's got to be silenced. A quick bullet is the answer. Now I want a volunteer to carry out the deed.'

There was a burble of discussion among those present but nobody raised their hand.

'Very well,' Buckthorn said, 'we'll have to draw straws. Whoever draws the short straw kills Snapp.'

After that he produced a flour sack and another man searched around for thick blades of grass. Out of our sight, these were trimmed, one shorter than the others, one for each person present, and these were placed in the sack with their ends exposed through the opening, drawn tight.

Buckthorn drew first — a long straw. Three others followed, all drawing long, then I was nudged forward. I reckoned the odds were still against me drawing the short straw. I certainly had no wish to kill an individual I'd never met and might, for all I knew, have told the truth when he'd claimed Buckthorn had gone for his gun first.

I gripped a straw, drew it out. My blood ran cold. It was short.

Deep down, I wondered if it had somehow been fixed, maybe through a sleight of hand, but I couldn't think how. I also wondered if this was some sort of test to measure my loyalty.

As the meeting dispersed, men going to their horses and riding away into the night, Buckthorn beckoned me over and apprehension quivered in me.

Although I am no short-ass, I felt like a dwarf as he towered over me.

'I'm glad I chose you for this work,' he said.

This seemed to confirm what I'd suspected, and my indignation gave me courage to speak out. 'Chose? I thought it was the luck of the straws!'

For the first and only time, I thought Buckthorn was lost for words. He opened his mouth but nothing came out, though it was only for a fleeting moment, then he said, 'You clearly don't understand the power of prayer. I prayed that God would choose you to carry out this task. It was His will. Keep in mind that Sam Snapp is an evil man who seeks to undo all the good work we've done.'

For another moment neither of us spoke. Once again he broke the silence: 'Snapp lives near Oak Grove Schoolhouse,' he explained. 'You must wait for him and keep hidden. When he appears aim true. Keep your face hidden. Nobody must suspect the Bald Knobbers. One shot must finish him, then get out fast. Stay hidden in the hills for a few days.'

'How do I recognize him?' I asked. 'I've never met him.'

He rested his powerful hand on my shoulder. 'Pray, my son. Remember, the Lord will show you the way.'

I nodded in acknowledgement. I guessed I was being tested. I only hoped the future would somehow guide me into doing the right thing.

★ ★ ★

Two days later, I took a profound risk. I ventured into town. I kept a low profile and an eye open for the marshal and any of his deputies. I harboured vague ideas of trying to contact Jessaka. How I longed to see her! But it was an early hour and she might not be at the hostelry, so I found a café on the banks of the White River. I still had some of the money left from that which Lum Boothe had paid me and I feasted on a fine meal of pork, potatoes, cabbage and corn bread and butter, followed by fried apples sweetened with sorghum, all washed down with strong black coffee. It was almost as good as the food Aunt Beth served.

A newspaper, several days old, had been left on my table. I picked it up, stuffed it inside my shirt.

Presently, I overheard a couple of men on the next table talking, and at the mention of the Bald Knobbers my ears pricked up. They were angry. Apparently, on a night of the previous week, the home of a family called Eden had been broken into by hooded men. The Edens had previously been heard speaking against the Knobbers. Mr and Mrs Eden and their two small children had been asleep, but they were dragged from their beds and murdered.

Of course Buckthorn had denied that the hooded murderers were Bald Knobbers and no proof had been found.

I was appalled by what I'd heard.

One of the men looked at me suspiciously. 'You ain't a Bald Knobber, are you?' he asked.

I gave my head a firm shake and said, 'No, sir.' He turned back to his companion.

As my head swirled with images of what had happened, I thought again of Jessaka. I felt gloomy as I realized that it was not only my own wishes that I had to consider, but also her safety. If I attempted to contact her, I would be placing her in jeopardy. Firstly, because she might be accused of associating with a Bald Knobber, and secondly she could still face the wrath of the law for helping me escape from jail.

I felt I had no option but to leave town.

Before I left the café, I asked the young waitress where Oak Grove Schoolhouse was. About a mile out of town, she said, along the VanZandt Road. I adopted a nonchalant attitude, pretending it was of little consequence.

★　★　★

For a week, I stayed in my river-gulley hideout, steeling myself for the ordeal ahead. I read every word in the newspaper I'd collected.

It was full of news about violence in Taney County. One correspondent was outspoken about the Bald Knobbers. The very name, he wrote, is a symbol of vindictiveness, treachery and outrage. The clan holds all decent citizens, who are not in its ranks, in a reign of force and terror. Its annals are written in the blood of innocent men and the wails of homeless widows and orphans.

★　　★　　★

I'd left matters for as long as I dared. I'd hoped my problems would go away, but they didn't. Finally, I made my move.

On the eighth day I was in the woods overlooking the schoolhouse. It only took me another ten minutes to locate the sprawling cabin where I surmised Sam Snapp lived. It was a lone residence in the vicinity. I watched as two children played in the yard fronting the place. Once, a man visited the privy; I guessed he was Snapp.

At that time, lightning forked the sky and thunder rumbled loudly and shortly heavy rain began to fall.

I sat slumped against the bole of a tree, soaking wet. I felt sick with the anxiety that had plagued me for the last week. Was I really going to kill this man who had done me no harm whatsoever, and who I'd never met in my life? Was he any more sinful than Buckthorn himself?

Of course, fear of Buckthorn still

dogged me. If I failed to carry out this murder, I reckoned I'd be doomed. If I fled from the locality I'd be hounded till my dying day. That was the level of dread I had for the man.

I cleaned my .44, checking that it was loaded. Of course, I knew it was, but I checked it just the same. It had five shells in the chamber but I hoped only one would be needed.

I was going through the motions of being a premeditating killer, ignoring what my heart and mind were telling me.

With the thunder still rumbling and the rain lancing down, I descended the slope towards the cabin, blanking any thoughts, any misgivings, from my head. In front of me, I saw the main window of the place. It showed yellow from a lamp inside. I also saw the movement of figures in what was obviously the main room. I was aware that while I had a view of the room, those inside would not see me. I drew my pistol and edged closer.

A man whom I didn't doubt was Sam Snapp was seated at the supper table with his children. He was spoon-feeding the youngest, a baby.

I swallowed hard.

It was then that some inner emotion resurfaced in me. I knew I could never murder this man in cold blood. Maybe gunning a man down in a fair fight is acceptable, or maybe when he's grievously wronged you, but when he's in his home, feeding his little ones . . . well, that was sure different.

I holstered my pistol and turned away, soaked to the skin and wondering how come I'd ever contemplated such a deed.

Perhaps Buckthorn was the one who needed killing.

14

Next morning I ventured out from my hideaway to hunt for game in the woods. I didn't have any luck and was about to return to the gulley when I heard a strange groaning sound. At first I thought it was an animal. It persisted for a minute and I decided to investigate.

Firstly, I encountered a bay horse in a clearing, pulling at the grass, then the groaning came again from further on. A moment later I found a white-haired old man, sprawled on the ground, holding his leg.

He looked alarmed as he saw me, but relaxed as I spoke to him in a soothing voice. 'What happened? You had a fall?'

He nodded glumly. 'Horse trod in a hole, threw me off her back. I figure my leg's broke. It sure hurts. I must've blacked out.'

I went to him and knelt down. Gently,

I felt his leg. He was scrawny-thin. 'Doesn't seem busted,' I said. 'Just twisted maybe.'

He gave a sigh. 'I got real trouble now.'

I thought, you're not the only one!

'My ol' woman's real sick. I figure she might be dyin'. I was on my way into town to fetch the doctor. But my horse trod in the damn hole.'

'I'm sorry,' I said.

He looked at me, his eyes showing sudden anxiety. 'Say, son, you ain't a Bald Knobber, are you?'

Once more I denied it. Lying was becoming a regular habit.

He reached out, his claw-like fingers grabbing my coat sleeve. 'Help me up,' he said, and I pulled him onto his feet. He winced with pain and cursed his leg.

'I can't go on,' he said. 'I can't leave my missus no longer. If she's gonna die, I guess I should be with her.'

A sudden light gleamed in his eyes. 'Say,' he said, 'would you do me a couple of favours?'

'What favours?'

'Maybe you could catch my horse

and help me get mounted, so I can go back home.'

'Sure,' I nodded.

'And the second favour,' he went on, 'is ride into town and fetch Doc Wilmer out for my wife. My name's Crosby. He knows us well. He'll know where to come.'

Uncertainty cut through me. I had little desire to return to town; even less to meet up with Wilmer again. Then I thought of my mother and her dying days. Now there was maybe another woman suffering in the same way.

Crosby gazed at me pleadingly. 'I can pay you,' he said, 'pay you real good.'

'I don't want your money,' I said.

'Then will you go?'

Hell's fires, I thought. I didn't ask my head to nod but it did.

Anyway, although it may seem crazy, fifteen minutes later found me heading for town, having left Crosby to return to his wife. I felt like a piece of flotsam, being tossed back and forth, manipulated by other people. And I figured that mighty soon, this piece of flotsam would become water-logged and sink.

I hit the outskirts of town just after noon. The place was a-bustle with the usual traffic. Keeping the brim of my hat pulled low, I followed along the street till I reached the medic's house. I knew I had an advantage over Wilmer. I had a gun, but I'd never known a doctor carry one.

I dismounted, hitched the roan close to the water trough. The main door of the place was open. I rang the bell, stepped inside and stood in the hallway. Almost immediately a young lady appeared and inquired my name.

I said, 'I'm here for Mrs Crosby. She's awful sick, maybe dyin'. Her husband would be mighty grateful if the doctor could go out to see her. I'll be on my way.'

I was turning to depart when Wilmer's voice came like a stab in the back.

'I think you'd better hold on a moment!'

My hand hovered over my gun, but I didn't draw it. Slowly I turned and faced the man whom I feared could be my stepping stone to the hang-rope. His eyes were bloodshot, but he seemed sober and to my surprise there was the faintest of smiles on his lips.

'Come inside,' he said, holding the door open to an inner room.

'I can't linger,' I said. 'How do I know you're not tryin' to trap me, like you did last time?'

'I promise you'll be safe,' he said, 'and there's somethin' else. I didn't kill your friend. There was nothin' I could do to save him. No doctor in the world could have done.'

I hesitated. This seemed crazy. Wilmer had been a raving drunk that night when Alfredo had died. Now, he seemed absolutely reasonable. I followed him into his surgery with some trepidation. Nobody else was there. He sat down at his table and motioned me to a chair.

'Doc,' I said, 'Mrs Crosby may be dyin'. You should get to her as quick as possible.'

He held up a pacifying hand. 'What I've got to say'll only take a minute.

From what Lum Boothe said when he was delirious, I guessed you were close by, maybe in a barn. When I left, I could have told the marshal and he'd've been after you like a shot. But I didn't give you away. Do you know why?'

I shook my head.

'It was because, just like you, I'd taken Buckthorn's oath. I swore I'd never wrong a brother member, and I figured if Buckthorn approved of you, you must be OK.'

'You mean you're a Bald Knobber?' I gasped.

He nodded, holding up his hand again, as if to preserve secrecy.

'Don't let me down,' he said. 'Keep out of trouble. I'll go to the Crosbys'. You leave first and get out of town before somebody recognizes you. I'll follow up in a few minutes. The Antis know I'm a Bald Knobber, so I've got to go carefully.'

I felt stunned by his revelation, but I wasn't going to look a gift horse in the mouth.

'How is Lum Boothe?' I asked.

'He's doin' fine,' he said, 'sittin' up and taking an interest.'

I backed out, unhitched the roan and mounted up. Soon the only evidence that I'd been in town, apart from the woman who greeted me, was the dust settling on the trail behind me.

I rode along the forest trail for about a quarter of an hour, aiming vaguely in the direction of the point where I'd encountered Crosby, when Wilmer caught me up and suddenly we were riding shoulder to shoulder. There was no talk between us, but it seemed incredible that this man whom I'd viewed as an enemy and a drunk was now my companion. But quite suddenly any satisfaction proved short-lived.

The shot cracked viciously from the shadowy trees alongside us, and I glimpsed Wilmer's horse rearing, throwing him from his saddle. I hauled the roan to a halt, cleared my feet from the stirrups and slid to the ground. As I did so, more lead went whizzing about my ears and I heard men shouting above the blast of gunfire. Our horses galloped off.

Hugging the ground, I crawled to where Wilmer was sitting up. Together we scrambled to the side of the trail, throwing ourselves down in the scrub. Guns were banging off, bullets chipping off splinters from the tree trunks about us. Death, it seemed, was just a whisper away.

I snatched my gun from its holster, straining my eyes to catch sight of our attackers. I realized that Wilmer was unarmed and I knew that our lives were hanging by a thread. Any chance of survival, it seemed, rested solely with me.

As further shots exploded, I caught the glimpse of flame from the thick foliage on the opposite side of the trail. I blasted off a shot in that direction, but had no way of telling whether I'd hit anybody. Nonetheless I'd seen enough to conclude that we were mightily outnumbered. I also realized that my own supply of ammunition was limited to no more than a dozen bullets.

'Who are they?' I gasped into Wilmer's ear.

'Damned Anti-Bald-Knobbers,' he growled.

Before I could make any response, a barrage of further gunshots had me ducking so low that I got a mouthful of earth. I spat it out and we edged back to gain cover behind the all-too-slender trunk of an aspen. The air reeked of gunsmoke.

And that was when I heard a rustling movement behind us and the sudden trembling in my guts told me we were lost. They were surrounding us.

'They've got us for sure,' Wilmer confirmed in my ear. 'Best thing we can do is give ourselves up. If we don't they'll gun us down.'

I was uncertain. I didn't know what they'd do with us if we surrendered, but of one thing I was sure. It wouldn't be pleasant.

Suddenly another shot blasted off. It

came from a heavy-calibre rifle. The lead breathed so close that another inch or so would have blown my head off. I decided Wilmer was right. I cupped my hands to my mouth and hollered, 'We give in. You got us for sure!'

From across the trail somebody called, 'Lay down your guns. Step out onto the trail with your hands raised.'

I exchanged glances with Wilmer and he nodded. I holstered my pistol, then, striving to quell my trembling, I climbed to my feet and walked into the open. Wilmer followed. For a moment we stood utterly exposed. Some maverick trigger-finger could blast us to eternity.

Six of our enemies emerged from the trees. All held guns that were levelled at us; all, that is, except one man who held a rope.

'What shall we do with them?' somebody asked.

The reply came without hesitation. 'Lynch the bastards!'

15

Wilmer spoke up with remarkable coolness. 'You know I'm a doctor. I was on my way to see Mrs Crosby. She's very ill, needs treatment. If you kill me, you'll probably kill her as well.'

'But you're a Bald Knobber,' one of our captors said. He was a thick-set man with bushy sideburns. 'You've terrorized this county so much that folks are movin' away. You don't deserve to live on this earth, so I say you and your sidekick hang now!' There was a burble of agreeing grunts. The man with the rope moved away, looking for a suitable branch from which to lynch us.

Wilmer seemed to take it in his stride, and maybe I, too, appeared calm. But inside, a feeling of hopelessness gripped me, and I prayed that when the rope choked me, I'd die instantly.

But matters were delayed. The tall

man who now came up behind us spoke with an authoritative voice; I guessed he was the leader of the group.

He said, 'If Mrs Crosby is sufferin' it would be un-Christian to deny her the doctor. I'll ride with him over to the Crosbys' place and we can decide what to do with him after he's treated her.'

'How about the other fella?'

I felt the sweat beading out on my body. My fate was hanging in the balance.

'If we lynch him,' the man behind me said, 'we'll be as bad as the Bald Knobbers. Remember we're a law and order organization. While I go over to the Crosbys', I want three men to escort this young fella over to Delaware and hand him over to the law. He'll get a trial and then he can be hung fair and legal if that's the decision.'

Some of the men were not happy with this, but they obviously respected their leader and three volunteers agreed to carry out the order.

I was grabbed and my hands were

tied behind my back. Meanwhile Wilmer spoke up, saying he needed his medical supplies, which were in his saddlebag. A man was despatched and returned shortly with the doctor's horse and my roan.

Within five minutes we were on our separate ways. The doctor and group leader to visit the sick woman; the majority of the Anti-Bald-Knobbers to their homes . . . and yours truly, accompanied by three escorts, to be handed over to the sheriff in Delaware, the seat of government. I had been given a stay of execution for the moment, but my prospects offered little cause for optimism.

It was a long, tedious ride along the White River Road, particularly so because my hands were tied. In the late afternoon, when we reached the town, folks lined the sidewalks, gawping at me as if I were some freak from a circus. The jail, a small hewed-log hut, stood in the public square. Oak planks covered the log walls. Inside were two cells, each with an inner and an outer door. Boilerplate iron strengthened the inner door, and all doors were secured with heavy padlocks. Without ceremony, I was bundled into the smaller cell.

I recalled my escape from the jail in Coltville, but this time there would be no Jessaka to help me, and when the door slammed behind me, I slumped onto the wooden bunk and let despair wash over me.

I wondered on what grounds I was being held. Had my earlier crimes somehow caught up with me? Or was the fact that I was a Bald Knobber enough to seal my fate? How did anybody outside the clan know I was a member? Later I was to discover, to my great disadvantage, that there were spies everywhere.

Now it appeared that the Bald Knobbers had fallen into total disrespect. The Antis had spread scorn and hatred for the clan and it was obvious that the law in Delaware shared these sentiments. All of which plunged me into the deepest jeopardy.

But a further shock awaited me; County Sheriff McHaffie visited me in my cell. He was a tall man with fierce eyes and, unusually, he was clean-shaven. He seemed to take delight in lashing me with his tongue, haranguing me with news that the Bald Knobbers had attempted to burn down the Taney County courthouse, for reasons best known to themselves. They were, he said, nothing but a band of outlaws, murderers and arsonists, who no longer represented innocent, law-abiding citizens. And Buckthorn was a bigot and the biggest hypocrite of them all.

When I could get a word in, I asked, 'What am I being charged with?'

The fact was I felt pretty sure I knew what my sins were. But what he said made the blood thump in my temples.

'As if you didn't know. You murdered a good man, Sam Snapp, gunnin' him down when he was eatin' supper with his kids. You're a damned bushwhacker!'

My mouth sagged. 'I never killed

him. I didn't know he was dead . . . '

He silenced me with an upraised hand. 'Try tellin' that to the judge,' he snapped. He glared at me with the intensity of a snake, then he stamped out, and I heard the rattle of a chain and keys as the door was secured.

For a moment anger welled up in me. What right had they to accuse me of killing Snapp when that was the one crime of which I was innocent? How ironic it would be if I was strung up for a murder I hadn't committed! My God, I'd accumulated enough guilt without having a faked-up charge pinned on me. But how was I going to prove that I hadn't killed Snapp? The fact that he was now dead astounded me. So was the news that he'd been gunned down in the way I'd once considered. And who had shot him, possibly minutes after I'd retreated from the scene?

As I calmed down, my brain buzzed with questions for which I had no answers. I wept, grinding my teeth with chagrin. I lay on the hard bunk and pleaded that some merciful blanket could be thrown over me and I could be whisked away to a paradise that had no past.

Eventually weariness took its toll and I slept.

It seemed much later when I heard the key rattling in the padlock and the door was thrown open. It must have been dark outside because, silhouetted in the light of a lantern, a figure loomed in the doorway. It was Wilmer. He acknowledged me as the door slammed shut behind him, then he slumped to the floor.

'The Anti-Knobbers are bastards,' he muttered. 'Worse than we ever were.'

I doubted he was right, but I shared his sentiments.

Presently, he told me how he'd been taken to the Crosbys' cabin, and how the place was swarming with mosquitoes. He'd diagnosed the wife as having malaria. He'd expected this all along; there'd been an outbreak of the disease in the locality. He'd had with him a supply of quinine, which he'd administered. He'd also fitted up mosquito netting over the woman's bed. He'd left Old Man Crosby with a further batch of quinine and instructed him to dose his wife with it five times daily. And that was all Wilmer could do. His escort, the apparent leader of the Anti-Bald-Knobbers, had forced him to leave at gunpoint and had subsequently handed him over to the law at Delaware. Wilmer told me that he had learned the Governor of Missouri had ordered the Bald Knobbers to be disbanded and that failure to do so would result in members being arrested and put on trial for offences committed. Buckthorn had denied being involved with the attempt to burn down the courthouse. He had also promised to disband his clan, but it was clear he had no intention of doing so. Now the governor had threatened to send in the militia to restore law and order.

The fact that Wilmer was a doctor made little difference. He would be tried as a vigilante and face the penalty if it could be proved he had committed a serious crime.

We were in total darkness and I guess we slept after that, each steeped in his own misery. Later, I awoke and heard sounds coming from the second cell. I concluded that other prisoners were being held. I wondered if they were Bald Knobbers, too.

The next two days passed in a haze of remorse. We were fed sparse rations and marched out, under heavily armed guards, to the privy. I got sight of the other prisoners. There were three of them. The face of one man was familiar and I realized I'd seen him at the first of Buckthorn's meetings and afterwards on one of the 'jobs', so I guessed the others were also Bald Knobbers. Locked away, during the rest of the time, we sweated out the long hours and dozed. I guessed that the powers that be were beavering away, dredging up evidence against us. Wilmer seemed to have run out of words for he was totally untalkative.

There were no windows in our cells but we sometimes heard sounds from outside. On the third night of our incarceration, I went to sleep fairly early, but was roused by Wilmer's snoring. I had been lying awake for a while, my mind mulling over depressing thoughts, when I heard a distant church clock strike twelve.

Later, I learned that this was a signal.

16

Suddenly I heard raised voices coming from outside. Immediately Wilmer was on his feet and we stood side by side in the darkness, straining to hear the words that were being exchanged.

'Open up the cells,' somebody yelled.

Sheriff McHaffie's defiance came clearly: 'I don't have no keys. Go to hell!'

There followed the vicious crack of a gun and we never heard McHaffie again. The thump of hoofs sounded, and Wilmer said, 'My God, sounds like a regiment out there in the square.'

Next, we heard a great hammering on the external door of the adjacent cell. It went on and on and at last a man cried, 'The padlock's too damned tough. We'll never smash it!'

'Give me the hammer,' came another voice and this time it was unmistakable.

It was Buckthorn. Seconds later the hammering sounded again, just once, and we knew that Buckthorn's brute strength had broken the lock. It obviously took next to no time for him to pry out the staple on the inner door because there were cries of jubilation as the inmates rushed out.

Wilmer shouted desperately, 'We're in here! Wilmer and . . . ' He trailed off. He'd forgotten my name.

He needn't have worried. Buckthorn was wielding his sledgehammer again, and the padlock gave almost immediately. When our door swung open, his giant body blocked out the light coming from outside firebrands. But I saw how his face, above his bandanna, was shining with sweat, how his eyes were wide like those of an insane man.

'Get out,' he yelled, making way for us.

We needed no second bidding.

Outside there were many shadowy horsemen, all with bandannas or flour sacks concealing their faces. I saw four deputies standing to one side, their hands raised, their faces sullen. I was grabbed beneath the armpits and hauled up behind a rider. I gripped him around the waist. The other released men were also doubling with riders. I saw Buckthorn mount his horse and wave his followers forward. We took off like the wind, the stars glinting in the heavens like beacons of freedom. Our cavalcade streamed across the square, down a street and out of town. It seemed like a crazy dream but it was one for which I was downright thankful . . . at the time.

Over the following hours we halted three times to rest the animals. We briefly dismounted, stretching our legs. At the third stop, I noticed that our numbers had thinned considerably. Most men had peeled off their masks. The man with whom I was riding was a stranger to me, but I thanked him for allowing me to share his horse.

He shrugged his shoulders and said, 'Where d'you want droppin' off?'

I hesitated, then said, 'Near Boothe's

farm.' It was the first place to enter my head. He nodded.

Next time we halted, there were only half a dozen of us left, including Buckthorn himself. He edged his horse alongside me and to my surprise thumped me on the back.

'Well done, son,' he said.

Surprised, I didn't use my brain. 'What for?' I blurted out.

'For killin' Snapp, of course. You've rid the world of a sinful man.'

I looked at him, wondering if he was somehow mocking me, but his face was serious.

I was about to deny that I had killed Snapp when I reined in my tongue. Instead I nodded. I had no wish to anger him. He reached out his great paw and I shook it.

'Now lay low for a while,' he said, and he turned his horse away.

True to my wishes, I was taken close to Boothe's farm. As I slid to the ground, I shook my benefactor's hand and he gave me a wave and rode off without a further word.

To the east, dawn was painting the peaks of the Ozarks pink. I debated what I should do and eventually decided that it could be safe to reacquaint myself with Lum and Aunt Beth. It was only as I approached the outbuildings of the place, when a cockerel unleashed its raucous greeting, making me start, that I realized how tense I was.

There was a light showing in the kitchen window. I went forward and entered to find Aunt Beth cooking something on the range. She immediately turned and her face lit up with joy as she saw me.

'Billy!' she cried, and she came over and gave me a great hug. And then Lum came into the kitchen, leaning heavily on his stick, his broad smile giving me all the welcome I needed.

Shortly, we were seated around the table and Aunt Beth was pouring out coffee. 'Pork, eggs and corn bread'll be ready in five minutes,' she proclaimed.

Lum leaned forward. His breathing

was very wheezy and I guessed he had a long way to go before he was fully fit — if he ever would be.

'That Sergeant McMahon was here a couple o' days back,' he said. 'He was askin' if we'd seen a youngster that was wanted by the military authorities for attempted armed robbery.' He looked at me from beneath his bushy eyebrows. 'That ain't you, is it, Billy?'

It was a direct question and I wasn't prepared for it.

'If I was,' I said, 'would you give me away?'

Aunt Beth started to speak but Lum cut across her. 'Not if you gave me an assurance that you'd never do it again. You worked hard for me and saved my life. I got no ill feeling towards you.'

'I'm doin' my very best to keep out of trouble,' I said, 'but . . . ' I explained to him how Buckthorn and his men had rescued us from the Delaware jail.

'Well,' he said, 'you stay loyal to the Bald Knobbers and they'll look after you.'

I nodded.

Soon, Aunt Beth dished up the food and a moment later we were tucking in.

We were seated in the kitchen with the outside door thrown open, letting in the fresh morning air.

When I looked up, I got a shock. Sergeant McMahon was crouched in the doorway, his gun levelled at me, a satisfied look on his swarthy face.

'I'm takin' you in,' he snarled. 'Stand up, hold your arms out in front o' you!'

With his free hand, he unfixed a set of handcuffs from his belt. He kept his pistol aligned with my belly button.

I rose, pushing the chair back with my legs. I eased away from the table, holding my arms out as instructed. I wondered if he was acting alone, or if he had a column of men in the yard. I thought not. My heart was thumping against my ribs. I sensed that the next few seconds could spell death for me. Some inner force was goading me into action.

As he stepped forward and attempted

to fasten the cuffs onto my wrists, his pistol wavered. I lashed out with all my strength, my arm thumping across his face. At the same time I drove my knee into his groin. He stumbled back, the gun flying from his grasp. I didn't delay. I knew the back way from the cabin.

By the time he had fumbled around to retrieve his pistol, I was sprinting down the slope towards the copse of cottonwoods. Later, I heard how McMahon fell as he set out in pursuit, tripped by Lum's extended stick.

I'd practically reached the trees when he burst through the back door of the place. Spotting me, he blasted off a shot, but it missed by yards. Seconds later, I was desperately forcing my way through thick, thorny wild rose and ferns, the canopy of branches over my head. But suddenly my flight came to an abrupt halt. My foot slipped beneath an unyielding root and I fell, face first, into a mass of prickly foliage. For a moment, I was stunned; the fear that he could now take me, shoot me dead if he chose, overwhelmed me.

Then I heard the floundering movement of a body ripping through the ferns, coming straight for me. I bunched my fists but knew I could do little to defend myself.

To my surprise, a grizzled javelina plunged into my field of vision. The creature saw me, raised its pig-like snout in surprise and then veered away to the left, blundering off, the sound of its progress receding.

I saw McMahon rush through the trees, his breath heaving, not sparing a glance in my direction. He immediately ran on in the wake of the sound, clearly believing it was me.

I knew now that I had a slim chance of escape, but I had to act quickly. I forced myself up, scrambling clear from the clinging thorns. My legs pumping with all the energy I could muster, I ran clear of the trees and up the slope towards the house. I was in the open, vulnerable to a bullet. I prayed that McMahon had not yet discovered his mistake.

To my relief, I reached the house and ran around its side. I had no wish to involve the Boothes any further in my troubles.

Emerging in the front, I saw McMahon's chestnut horse hitched to a rail. Grunting with relief, I ran to it, unfastened its reins, got my foot in the stirrup and hauled myself into the saddle. I rammed hard with my heels and we were away.

If McMahon saw me depart, I couldn't tell. By now he must have discovered that what he was chasing had four legs and tusks. But one thing was certain: he'd be combusting with rage, not only caused by the fact that I'd eluded him, but also because his horse had been stolen. And I was to learn, to my misfortune, that the sergeant was not a man to resign himself to humiliation.

17

McMahon's chestnut was lively and fresh. This led me to believe that the animal had recently rested, perhaps while the sergeant had been watching for me to show up at the farm. Now, as well as me acquiring his animal, there was a fine Winchester rifle in the saddle scabbard.

I wondered if McMahon had commandeered one of Lum's horses and was coming after me. I gazed back across the slopes I'd traversed but I saw no dust, no dogged rider. I hoped that McMahon had not chosen to vent his rage on the Boothes.

I had little idea where I was heading. My main concern was to get away. Eventually I crossed over the crest of a hill and that was when I saw the ranch in the valley below, with its windmill and corralled horses. There was an arch straddling the trail leading into it. I could just make out its lettering — God's Pastures.

I guessed it then, guessed that here was the domain of Nathaniel Buckthorn! Who else would choose such a pious name for their outfit?

Somehow, an obscure fate had guided me to this place. I would never know the reason why.

But if I harboured hopes of finding sanctuary here, I suffered a severe setback. Maybe I was too engrossed with my thoughts because I failed to notice how pitted with holes the slope before me was. Sensing the nearness of the horses in the corral, the chestnut trotted forward briskly and promptly plunged his left foreleg into a hole. Withdrawing it, he jerked up with such vigour that I lost my grip on the saddle and slithered backwards. With the animal pounding on, I hit the ground and was unable to pull my foot clear of the stirrup. As I was dragged along my leg got an almighty wrench, agony shot through my knee and I knew immediately that it was dislocated.

This wasn't the first time I'd been thrown from a horse, but I guess it was the most disastrous.

When my foot came clear of the stirrup, I was left sprawled on my back, dazed and suffering awful pain, only fleetingly aware that the chestnut had galloped on. Maybe it was his revenge for having been purloined.

I must have fainted.

When my senses returned and I tried to move, the agony radiating upward from my knee was so bad that I would gladly have submitted to amputation in that moment. I cried out, my head dropping back. Then I felt something clawing into my shoulder. It was a hand. I opened my eyes and realized that a man was stooping over me. Behind him was his horse, along with another man who remained mounted.

I recognized them. They were both Bald Knobbers. The man who had given my shoulder a shake was Joe

McGill and his companion was Jack Middlemass.

'What happened?' McGill inquired.

I was angry, both with myself and with the pain that tortured me.

'Horse threw me,' I muttered, 'then hightailed it.'

'Best leave him lyin' there,' Middlemass said. 'Let him recover in his own good time, eh?'

'No,' McGill countered, slipping his hand beneath my armpit. 'We best get him down to the house. He's a friend of Nathaniel.'

'Not really,' Middlemass said.

But McGill was insistent. He helped me up onto my feet, or rather onto my foot, for I could not put my left leg to the ground. Wincing with pain, I was helped down the slope.

'We'd better make haste,' Middlemass said impatiently, 'before those soldier-boys get here.'

'Soldiers,' I grunted, 'you saw soldiers?'

'Sure,' McGill said. 'We saw 'em a

half-hour back, maybe twenty militia-men. They just stopped to rest their horses, but I guess they was headed this way.'

I groaned, but I hobbled on a little faster. Middlemass rode along behind us, leading McGill's mount.

When we reached the flatter ground the going became easier. We passed the corral and as we approached the house, Buckthorn appeared on the veranda. His expression was bleak. 'What's happened?' he demanded.

'We were on our way here when we found the kid,' McGill explained. 'He'd fallen off his horse and busted his leg, I guess.'

'He shouldn't have been comin' here,' Buckthorn said. 'He had no right.'

'Well, we best get him inside,' McGill said. 'We spotted some soldiers a few miles up the valley. It looked as though they was headed this way.'

Buckthorn's face took on the look of a thunder-cloud. Had he been a cursing man he'd have probably turned the air blue, but he remained tight-lipped. After a moment he said, 'Bring him inside, then.'

Within a minute, I had been rested down on a couch in the big main room of the ranch house. Mrs Emily Buckthorn, a portly woman, appeared and made sympathetic noises at my injury. She fetched a pair of scissors and began to cut a slit in my pants. This annoyed me, for they were good pants. She winced as she saw the mess my knee was in.

Meanwhile, McGill stood at the window, gazing out, I guessed, for a sight of the military. Buckthorn and Middlemass became engaged in serious conversation.

'Governor Marmaduke threatened to send the militia in unless the Bald Knobbers were disbanded,' Buckthorn said. 'But I told him we would disband.'

McGill said, 'Well, I guess he didn't believe you, and there's been plenty more incidents since then.'

'They've not been done by us,' Buckthorn declared, 'but every outlaw in the county has jumped on the bandwagon and blackened our name.'

'Nobody believes it weren't us,' Middlemass muttered, 'certainly not the governor. Talk in town was that he wanted all vigilantes arrested.'

'This is not God's will.' Buckthorn thumped the table in anger. 'We must resist.'

When I glanced down, the sight of my knee was far from reassuring. The kneecap seemed to have slipped sideways and the whole area was swollen up and bruised. With gentle fingers, Emily Buckthorn attempted to restore the kneecap to its rightful position, but the pain was so intense that I couldn't bear it. She gave up and instead wound some bandage around for support. Then she brought me a stout walking stick.

She said, 'We haven't got a crutch, but this may help. You must get to a doctor as soon as possible. I shall pray for you. Now you rest, try to get your strength back.'

I thanked her but I wasn't in the

mood for rest. Apart from my wreck of a leg, I felt my strength had returned, but talk of the military coming filled me with alarm.

I tried to rise, but she pressed me down and I gave in. Perhaps the soldiers won't show up, I thought. That seemed to be the best I could hope for.

But now Buckthorn was pacing the floor, muttering beneath his breath. Maybe he was praying. Middlemass had slumped into a chair, dragging nervously on a cigarette. For a while the only sound was the ticking of the fine grandfather clock that stood in the corner of the room. I tried to doze but I was too agitated.

It was about twenty minutes later when I saw McGill's back come suddenly erect as he gazed through the window. His hissed warning cut through the room like a butcher's knife.

'They're here!'

Buckthorn lifted his gun-belt down from a hook and strapped it on. Middlemass stubbed out his smoke and came to his feet. I, too, forced myself up from the couch and stood on one leg, leaning on the stick.

'There's a column o' maybe twenty riders,' McGill said. 'They're pullin' somethin'; looks like a cannon.'

Middlemass unleashed a deep sigh.

Buckthorn stepped out through the doorway and stood on the veranda. McGill followed, standing just behind him. I hobbled to the window, gazed out. The line of bluecoats was approaching at a fair pace, moving down onto the flatter ground. As they drew closer I could see the officer at their head. He was mounted on a fine bay horse and there was about him a marked flamboyance. Two more officers followed him. When they reached a point about a hundred yards from the ranch yard, the main column halted, but the three officers continued to ride forward towards the house. On reaching it, they reined in before the veranda to confront Blackthorn.

I edged away from the window, but the voices carried clearly.

'Good afternoon to you, sir. I am Colonel Mileson of the Missouri State Militia. Am I right in saying that you, sir, are Nathaniel Buckthorn, leader of the organization known as the Bald Knobbers?'

Buckthorn's words showed an edge of defiance. 'You are correct, and what business have you here today?'

'We are acting on the Territorial Governor's authority. I have orders to arrest you and others of your group. Will you please hand over your gun and submit to my command.'

Buckthorn's response came hard as rock. 'Over my dead body!'

Mileson said, 'Then you leave me no option but to use force.'

For a moment Buckthorn seemed taken aback, but then he said, 'I suggest we make a bargain. I have here a young man, an outlaw and a murderer, whom the army are huntin'. Take him, and the rest of us can reach some agreement.'

I gasped with dismay. Right then, if I'd had a gun, I'd have shot the betraying son of a bitch in the back. I wondered since when he had known about me and why he had played me along.

The colonel's answer came firmly. 'I will not bargain with you. My orders are to arrest you all.'

Half-hidden by the window's curtain, I got a view of Buckthorn's broad back. I saw him draw his pistol and point it at the officer. 'We will not submit,' he cried out. 'The Lord is on our side.'

Mileson sat erect in his saddle, unfazed by the threat of the gun. With his sweeping moustache and his blond hair cascading down beneath his campaign hat, he could have been George Custer, had the latter not gone to his grave ten years back. Quite coolly he said, 'If you will not submit, then I repeat that I shall have to use force — '

'May you rot in hell!' Buckthorn interrupted.

'I think that unlikely,' Mileson retorted. 'Now if Mrs Buckthorn is present in the house, please send her out. She will be safe and treated with the utmost courtesy, then conveyed to a place of her choice.'

I watched Emily Buckthorn bristle with anger. Suddenly she shrieked out so loudly that everybody heard. 'I'll not go!'

The colonel dipped his head in acknowledgement. 'Then I fear you must all face the consequences. There is no alternative.'

Still ignoring the threat of Buckthorn's gun, he turned his horse, and his companions followed him as he rode back to the point where the main column was mustered. Soon we heard a non-com bawling orders.

18

McGill asked, 'What d'you reckon they'll do, Cap?'

Buckthorn didn't answer but Middlemass spoke up. 'They got field artillery. If they turn that on us, we're gonners! I say we get out the back o' this house before we're all blasted to bits.'

Buckthorn swung around. 'I'll not be bullied,' he exclaimed. 'I will put my faith in the Lord.'

'Surely, for the sake of your wife,' Middlemass pleaded, 'you must make her leave!'

Buckthorn glared at him but his words seemed to sink in.

'Very well,' he said, 'take my wife. Make sure she's safe.'

Emily Buckthorn started to protest but he hushed her into silence. Middlemass grabbed her arm and hustled her from the room. McGill looked wild and uncertain, but after a moment he had made up his mind. 'I'll stay with you, Cap,' he said. It struck me that he was a man of outstanding loyalty.

As for me, I seemed to have been forgotten. I knew I no longer had any allegiance to Buckthorn, only contempt. He'd been willing to hand me over to the military; for that I would never forgive him. I no longer wished to be a sitting duck for a man I no longer respected. Using the stick, I hobbled across the room, went through the kitchen and out through the back door.

That was when an almighty boom sounded and a heavy shell screamed over the house and exploded into the earth fifty yards to my front. The blast hit me, made me stagger. Later I learned it was a warning shot, hoping to break Buckthorn's nerve. Now, with horror, I realized the shell had landed close to where Middlemass and Buckthorn's wife were stumbling along. At first, as the dust cleared, I could see no sign of them. I hobbled forward.

Suddenly my gaze cottoned on to the two figures lying on the ground.

Almost forgetting my own pain, I reached the woman first. To my relief she forced herself into a sitting position. Her face was blackened yet ashen, her dress in shreds. She drew a shaking hand across her forehead, then she looked at me with dazed eyes and I somehow knew that she would survive. Soon, I was helping her to her feet. She was a strong woman. She must have been to put up with her pious husband.

Supporting each other, we staggered across to where Middlemass was sprawled on his back. He appeared dead. There was a huge chunk of metal embedded in his chest. As I leaned forward to examine him, the cannon boomed again accompanied by the scream of metal through air. Both Emily Buckthorn and I ducked, but this time the shell exploded in the front yard of the house. The army gunners were bracketing the place. Where would the next shell fall?

I'd almost forgotten about Middlemass, but now he groaned. He was alive but only just. How on earth he survived with his chest caved in by the hunk of metal was a miracle. I reckoned he wouldn't last long. There was nothing we could do for him.

We had to get away, but before we moved on I relieved Middlemass of his pistol and tucked it into my belt. He would have no need of it now, but I might.

Mrs Buckthorn would have remained with him, but somehow I urged her onward. Ahead of us was a fringe of cottonwoods beyond which I guessed was a river.

We'd almost reached the trees, when a man stepped out from them and blocked our way. It was Sergeant McMahon and his gun was raised. Grappling with my stick and the woman's arm, I made an effort to draw the pistol from my belt, but I stood no chance. His gun spat flame and an agonizing impact slammed into my chest, hurling me back with the woman's scream scorching in my ears. I tried to snatch breath, but it felt as if an iron band was girding my lungs. As I exhaled, blood gurgled from my mouth.

I heard his boots pacing closer. He loomed over me, his lips drawn back, his teeth bared like a wolf. He raised his gun, ready for another shot, but he didn't press the trigger. Instead his words came with the impact of bullets.

'You escaped me once, made me look a fool, but not this time!'

I lost my way, smothered by an oblivion that was blacker than death.

19

Of course, my experiences in Missouri took place many years ago, but I have related them as well as my memory permits. After McMahon shot me, as I fought my desperate battle to stay alive, thoughts of escape were out of the question. I was close to death as the military conveyed me back to the infirmary at Fort Sibley. There, an army surgeon removed the bullet and placed a splint on my leg. One of my lungs was ruined and I was to limp for the rest of my life.

From what I could gather, the soldiers charged into the house after the second cannon shot and captured Nathaniel Buckthorn. He was sent for trial by the civil authorities at Coltville. He faced charges of inciting murder and violent unrest, but he had covered his tracks well and there was a lack of firm evidence. Furthermore, the majority of the jury were former Bald Knobbers. As a result, he was acquitted and walked from court a free man, much to the chagrin, I'm sure, of Colonel Mileson and those who hated him. None the less, he still had many supporters and was soon voicing ambitions of running for the position of Taney County Sheriff.

As for me, after some weeks in the post infirmary, I was judged fit enough to stand before a military tribunal on charges of attempted armed robbery.

Appointed as defending officer was a young Lieutenant Endersby, a conscientious man who listened to my story intently and made copious notes.

When the trial opened the judge advocate, a Major Belden, read out the charges in a pompous voice.

I pleaded not guilty as instructed by Lieutenant Endersby.

Major Dyar, the grim-faced prosecuting officer, then painted a very black picture of me, reminding the tribunal of General Sherlock's order that all bandits should be exterminated, either by bullet or hang-rope.

Proceedings dragged on with Sergeant McMahon adding his evidence with all the pent-up hatred he felt for me. Finally, Lieutenant Endersby pleaded my case in the most dramatic and passionate way, extolling how my mother had died and how I had been under extreme influence to fall into a life of crime. Furthermore, the offences I had committed had been minimal and had been brought about only by my wish to survive.

A short adjournment was called after Endersby stood down. When the tribunal reconvened, the president read out the verdict. To my amazement, and due to the fact that I was still only sixteen years of age, I was acquitted. But I was to be handed over to the civil authorities to face further prosecution.

I swung round to give Lieutenant Endersby a grateful handshake, but he was turning away, his duty done.

Two weeks later I was conveyed to the fire-damaged courthouse in Coltville to stand trial on the charges of murdering

Samuel Snapp, attempting to burn down the marshal's office and escaping from custody. I was outraged by the murder charge, but I realized I had virtually nothing to support my plea of innocence.

Evidence for the prosecution was gleaned from the lips of Jack Middlemass, who had somehow retained a failing grip on life following his terrible injury. He had stated that he'd followed me for some days and had witnessed the killing, having seen me departing from Snapp's residence with a gun in my hand. But now he himself was near to death at the Coltville infirmary.

Oh, how I wished I'd had Lieutenant Endersby to defend me! Instead I was allotted a stern-faced lawyer, Jason Beavins, who wore a pince-nez that kept dropping from his nose and gave me little hope in my attempt to avoid the full penalty. My claim of being under age would hold little water, for Judge Stevens, who was to sit in judgement, had recently sentenced a youngster to the rope in Colorado.

I was plunged into the deepest depression as I awaited my trial. Many melancholy thoughts flooded my brain. If only I'd realized the true gravity of what I'd allowed myself to be led into. I didn't blame Alfredo for my troubles. He'd done his best to dissuade me from accompanying him but I'd insisted. Had I not been so desperate, I might never have heard of the Bald Knobbers or been witness to some of the terrible deeds they committed. And Buckthorn would never have tasked me with committing murder. How wonderful it would have been to go back over my life and erase the most hideous events!

I was at my lowest ebb for infection from my wound set in, bringing with it debilitating pain. Nonetheless, I was deemed fit enough to stand trial and maybe sufficiently strong to face a hanging. And so I was arraigned before Judge Stevens; the verdict seemed pre-judged from the start.

Sam Snapp had been an upright, clean-living widower who had looked after his children with the utmost care.

Now, the affidavit of the dying Jack Middlemass was totally damning, and the plea of mitigation from my defending lawyer did nothing to sway the minds of the jurors away from any verdict but guilty. In consequence I faced the dreaded sight of the judge placing the black cap upon his head and speaking words that are seared into my memory like a scar.

'Billy Stark, you have undergone a fair trial and have been found guilty of the murder of Sam Snapp. The sentence for such a crime is unequivocal. At a time convenient to the authorities you will be taken to a place of execution and hanged by the neck until you are dead.'

I was led back to my cell in a state of numbness.

I prayed on my knees that night to the adjudicator in the sky who would be my final judge. I prayed that all my sins might be forgiven.

But in the event, my resignation to a hanging was premature. Another man's death-bed confession proved my salvation.

Being so close to his heavenly Maker, Jack Middlemass, a Roman Catholic, had withdrawn his previous affidavit on the grounds of being untrue. To Father Cavanagh, he had made his final confession.

Apparently Nathaniel Buckthorn had not trusted me to carry out his order to kill Snapp and had instructed Middlemass to follow me and ensure the assassination was done, saying that it was the will of God. He had watched me approach Snapp's cabin and peer in the window, then turn back. Rain had been pouring down.

In anger, he had subsequently gone to the cabin himself and shot Snapp.

The sound of the gun was obliterated by a great clap of thunder.

He hoped that in replacing his affidavit with his true confession, he would save the life of an innocent man and go to his grave with a clearer conscience, which presumably he did.

The church minister conveyed the evidence to a reconvened court and, to my overwhelming relief, Judge Stevens quashed the death penalty but sentenced me to two years' imprisonment for the lesser offences.

★　★　★

I spent the two years in the Missouri Penitentiary, firstly in the infirmary until my wound was completely healed over, and the pain in my leg partially relieved. After this, I worked in the prison library, cataloguing books and making myself as generally useful as I could. I also found time to study many of the books.

When eventually I was free, I went to the hostelry in Coltville and inquired after Jessaka. Apparently her family had sold up and moved to Florida. Jessaka herself had married a teacher and was said to be very happy, with a baby on the way.

Of course I was gutted. But what

right had I to expect a girl I'd only met for a few minutes to be as smitten with me as I was with her? Even though she'd taken the gravest risk in enabling me to escape from jail. I'd thought . . . well, maybe I was wrong.

Gradually, I recovered from my regret. Perhaps it was the final part of the punishment for all the trouble I'd got myself into.

I'd moved to Rimrock Springs, a town in Texas, firstly taking a job as a bartender, then becoming a deputy to the town marshal. Within five years I took over as marshal, in which post I served for thirty-five years, somehow overcoming the handicap of a useless lung and a crippled leg.

In the early days, many volunteers had joined the Bald Knobbers with the sincere wish to drive transgressors from the county, but their ranks had been supplemented by cruel and greedy sinners. Buckthorn's high-sounding ambitions had changed to a reign of terror. Now, those who had been associated with the

Bald Knobbers melted into the obscurity of their previous lives but it took many years before real law and order prevailed.

Sometimes now, in my retirement, I take from my drawer the newspaper, yellow with age, which published details of the event that proved to be the closing chapter for the Bald Knobbers. It reads:

'On Sunday last, Nathaniel Buckthorn, who was tipped to be a representative in the State Legislature, was leaving church when he was accosted by a stranger who had just ridden into town. Both men were armed with pistols, and for a moment they stood glaring at each other. The newcomer was heard to accuse Buckthorn of ruining his life. Buckthorn replied that he had no proof.

'The stranger then went for his gun, but Buckthorn, being a former gunslinger, drew first and felled the other man with a shot to the chest. From the ground, the stranger fired a shot which caught Buckthorn in the forehead.

'With the two men sprawled in the dust, passers-by rushed to the scene and discovered that both were dead.

'A photograph of the corpses, taken by R.A. Nash, is published below.'

Sometimes I can hardly believe the evidence of the camera, for there, lying in grim repose, is Nathaniel Buckthorn, looking, for all the world, as if he will suddenly rise and bludgeon again the ears of his supporters with his bigotry of fire and brimstone, claiming all his deeds were in God's name when in truth they were in the Devil's.

But it is the other man who draws my foremost interest. If he knew that his shot had killed the monster he hated, he would have died satisfied. The man was my father.

THE END